Female Domination and The loving Cruelty

The Loving Cruelty complete Saga

Stacy Yang

Female Domination and
The Loving Cruelty

By Stacy Yang

∞ ∞ ∞

Academy

The Femdom Academy, as it is known today, was indeed old. It had gone thru many changes and many names over the years. It began as a column in a pulp magazine written by the authority on such matters, Mistress Jessica Yang. She was of mixed heritage living the first years of her life very poor in the slums outside Hong Kong. She herself was sold into slavery at the tender young age of ten to a wealthy man who traveled all over the world. He was not a pedophile, and never laid a hand on her. Instead, he saw the value of having the opportunity to raise a child, and he educated her about the world, but he also wanted a personal attendant he could train properly. He was a good man until the day he died when Jessica was 25 years old. As he had never married, calling it a "Fools folly", he had no children. He had left the bulk of his fortune, and property, to her. She mourned him terribly. He had educated her himself, and he was a visionary. Her mission in life was to honor his legacy. She would become the educator. She would do her part to improve the world, most of which she had seen for herself by the age of 22, thanks to him. Also, thanks to him, she had the tools to do it. She now owned a publishing company he had purchased, as well as many other companies. She owned so much property all over the world she was the single richest woman on earth. Her worth was in the billions, but how much exactly was hard to know at any given moment. The will he had left was not only iron clad, but it was also intelligently strategic to protect her. Several greedy men tried to strip her of her wealth and property. She crushed them all. Not simply defeating their efforts but destroying them with relentless attacks in all areas of their lives. Soon, no one tried.

The 'Renovation clinic' was built on her 1000-acre estate in north Nevada near Lake Tahoe in the early 1920's. She capitalized on the recent trend and the liberal laws making Reno Nevada the easiest place for a woman to be granted a divorce. Women from all over the country would come to divorce their husbands for a multitude of reasons. Jessica offered an option to the women who desired to keep their husbands, to have them transformed. If the husbands would agree to the rehabilitation program, the women would be returned a man nothing like the one that they had surrendered. The wives themselves were required to take training as well, but for them it was more like being at a resort learning skills to keep their newly reeducated husbands in line.

The term Reno-vated was born. The program, although changed over time, remains much the same. The principles it was founded on being sound, effective and appealing. Femdom is the slang for Female Domination. It was fast becoming popular across the world, and thanks to technological advents such as the internet, as well as the feminist movement, interest has grown like never before.

Mistress Jessica had not had any children, and she was never married. Before her death in 1971 at the age of 81, she had liquidated all of the property and holdings globally except for the 1000-acre estate in Nevada. She developed a foundation that would insure the existence of the institution for future generations of women. If it was cared for properly, managed wisely, it could go on indefinitely.

"Femina Virum Dominamini"

were the words carved into stone with 10 inch high roman gothic letters on the brick and stone adorned archway above the entrance to the "Big house". It could be translated to mean "Women rule over man".

The big house was a mixture of offices and sitting rooms. There was a large ballroom downstairs, a game room, the old kitchen which was still a kitchen, but is not used for daily food service. It is used more as a break room or prep room for snacks if there were a party. There were actually several gourmet kitchens now, one in each house.

There was a Mistress for each house who was responsible for several training Doms who did the bulk of the training. Usually 3 or 4, but sometimes as few as 1 or 2. Some of the training Doms are there to learn skills before setting out as a "Pro Dom", and in that respect those women are the finest Pro Doms who are very well respected and command the highest levels of fees. Certification by the academy does not come easy. It might take years. Only once a training Dom has displayed her worth is she certified. Many do not go on to be certified, or to be a pro Dom, but use the knowledge personally to dominate men.

Still others see it as a calling and remain at the academy, making the world better, one man at a time. Each of the women serving as training Doms had to be screened before even learning about the academy. They are approached with the opportunity, in a controlled way.

A few have been referred. But there are NO self-applicants in the training Dom program. This policy avoided unwanted attention, and helped to insure quality Doms, suited to the mission.

There seemed to be a lot of them lately. Good ones, too. Not so long ago it was a difficult task to scout and recruit potential Doms. A sign of the times, and the need for the institution. Male enrollment is at an all-time high. The trend is definitely upward.

From the desk of Jessica Yang,

The following is a guide to help maintain the training your male has received, and a list of best practices.

Congratulations, your male has been trained and is now ready for service to you. There is possibly no better lifestyle than that of a Woman who has a well-trained male, and you are sure to be the envy of your peers.

It is important that you maintain dominance. He will test you. He will get complacent if you are. You can lose control. Disobedience first happens in thought, then in speech. And finally, then in actions. He is well trained now, but unless you assert your authority from the very beginning upon arriving home, you will be on a path that will undo his training. I encourage you to follow these basic guidelines from the very minute you get home.

- Be very clear about your expectations. Tell him your rules. Manage every minute of his day at first and leave nothing up to his interpretation. This could be hard at first, but it will get easier as time goes on. Keeping to the program is critical to your male's performance.

- Keeping him nude, whenever it is possible, is a constant reminder of his status for both of you. It will seem weird at first, but you will become used to it. It also makes it easier to inspect him, and provides easy access to punishing him, or teasing him. If he must dress for guest, or for work, you should choose his clothing. You should control every aspect of his appearance right down to the order he puts his clothing on.

- Keeping him in a chastity device ensures there are not any opportunities for him to pleasure himself. He needs you for that. So, keep your key around your neck.

- Punish him. Let nothing slide. If he is perfect, punish him anyway. Punish him cruelly and often, but always provide after care and soothe him. Let him know you care about him but let him know you have no problem punishing him. Punishment comes in many forms and gives you an opportunity to be creative. Standing in a corner or writing lines are examples suitable for minor infractions. Have a notebook just for his lines, don't throw any away. Men are visual, and seeing his progress reinforces your training.

- Remove all choice. He is to seek out your direction in every matter, even ones where he may have the most knowledge about the subject. You now run the show and you don't need him making choices. You control the money, but you might have him pay the bills. He doesn't get to decide how much money to pay to the credit cards. He doesn't get to open accounts. You send him shopping with a list, he doesn't get to deviate from your list, and if he forgets items from the list, punish him. Make sure that never happens again. He doesn't get to spend money. If you allow him an allowance, make it very small and give him cash. Always demand receipts. Making him get a receipt for small purchases is humiliating.

- Remove all privacy. Inspect any space you allow him to use. Open every drawer, look in every box. Throw away things you think are clutter, better yet make him do it in front of you. He is to give you access to his email and all online activity. If he has social media accounts, you may allow him to keep it, but you are the one who views it. He should not be allowed to maintain any distraction from his service to you. Once you have his passwords, change them all and don't tell him what you changed them to. You might allow him to view or use the computer, but he will need you to log in for him and supervise his activity.

- Use him for your pleasure, you get pleasure even if he is denied. Use him for your grooming, he can bath you and shave your legs. Use him to rub your feet, or full body massage. Use him as a stool if you need to sit down for a minute or prop your feet up while you are sitting down. Use him to hold something for you. He should be what you need him to be, where you need him to be it.

- Be clear about protocols and insist that he maintains your standards in any circumstance. I suggest you develop nonverbal communications, perhaps hand signals, for use when in mixed company.

- Free time for your male is a good thing that can become destructive. Keep it to a minimum. Make it a reward and a real luxury. "Extra" time is better spent by him reflecting on you and anticipating your needs, not by watching a football game or playing a video game.

- Have him keep a journal. Have him write in it each night.

Loving Cruelty

Queen Melissa received a gift of a male slave from a friend while on a visit to Waco. Everyone knows how much she enjoys getting and testing a new slave, which she normally buys at auction. It was a thoughtful gift. She hasn't had the time to attend an auction for quite some time. Somehow it showed, she supposed. Was she being hostile to people?

She was called "Queen Melissa" by her deceased husband of 5 years. The title stuck. He had been her submissive. Her first. Her love for the BDSM community came later. Nobody she had ever met was actually a slave in the BDSM community. But willingly assuming the role appealed to a lot of people. She had been shocked to learn that. Removing choices from people simplified life for them. Having total power over someone appealed to her.

She would not have bid on, much less purchased a slave this old or in this condition. She was told he is newly trained and inexperienced. She hates getting a slave right out of academy. She prefers references. Skilled slaves. But, to not accept the gift is rude. Also, she does not have a servant traveling with her on this trip. He may be of use.

She decides to take some time testing this new slave, who now only has the number 12 for a name, to see his level of training and obedience. Not to mention his ability to please, or to take punishment.

It may be entertaining to find out. He isn't bad looking, there could be potential. Perhaps she will name him and keep him. If he proves worthy. She could always auction him off later if he doesn't.

Either way, she has a couple of days to put him thru the paces. She does this with all of her new slaves. She has a bit of an evil smile as the sadistic part of her awakens, this is her favorite part........

"Let me see what I have here." she said walking around him. Looking him up and down. "Take off your clothes so I can get a look at you." He begins to strip without a word. He hasn't said a word yet. Good, she thinks to herself. He also kept his eyes on the floor. He has had some training. "Raise your head and look at me when I am talking to you." and he does exactly that. Nice eyes she thought to herself. She liked blue eyes.

He kept his eyes on her while he undressed. He wasn't wearing that much. She told him to place his clothes in the bottom drawer of the dresser. She eyed his ass as he bent at the waist to achieve that. He turned around to face her when he was finished.

He was about 5'10", a little overweight but he had muscles. He wasn't tone, though. Room for improvement she thought to herself. He was wearing a stainless-steel chastity cage. His cock was straining in it, she could see. She had been given the keys on a small key chain with a little leather tag that had the number "12" on it. Now she could see that it was for the lock attached to the cock cage.

She pointed to a spot on the carpet for him to stand at and softly said "One". He responded immediately moving to the spot and smoothly achieving the number one position, legs spread, hands on head, back straight. This really was the best position for inspection. She walked up to him; he did not move. Placing her left palm at the top of his chest just below his neck she grabbed the cock cage in her right hand and softly pulled down on it. She pushed back on the spot under her left hand.

The cage was warm with his heat, and he let out a sigh of maybe pleasure, maybe pain. then she moved her right hand to grab his balls. She squeezed softly. He gave the same sigh with each squeeze. Then she moved her left hand to his throat and put it around, as best she could with her small hands, and squeezed. "These belong to me now, do you understand?" she said at him firmly and when he answered "Yes, I understand." in a strained voice, she held on just a heartbeat or two longer then let go. She ran her left hand down his chest, along his right side around to his back sliding down to his ass cheek. After giving that a firm squeeze, she slapped it, then turned her back to him and walked over to a chair and sat down.

"The next time you open your mouth to speak to me, whatever the reason, you will address me properly as your Queen." she spoke slowly in a low and soft voice, one of that sounded like she was talking about the weather. Not one of scorn or anger. "If you do not, you will lose your speech privileges." She was looking right at him. "Do you understand me?" she asked him "I do, my Queen. I understand you." his voice was also calm, and that made her smile. She had a nice smile, he thought. A cute face with piercing eyes, full red lips and he thought she might have been 40ish. Maybe younger. She smelled good too. It was clear she used expensive perfume. Her body was nice. She was on the short side with small hips and very large breast. She was wearing tights that hugged her legs and a white blouse that had red print of birds of paradise flowers on it. It had sleeves that did not make it to her wrist, which both had several gold bracelets.

"Two" she said not pointing or looking at anything besides her nails. He assumed the number two position, kneeling, back straight, legs spread, hands on head. She was most delighted that he responded so well, and that he knew the positions by number on command. It is hard to teach, sometimes harder to learn, and just all around a pain in the ass. " Good. Good," she said " Now, I want your hands behind your back." And, as if he knew what she was going to ask for, he smoothly lowered his hands behind his back, but otherwise staying at position two.

"I don't like cowards. Do not avert your eyes again. Do not ever hang your head unless directed by me to do so. As MY slave you will conduct yourself with dignity at all times." she maintained her calm and a rather soothing tone. " We will go over my rules for you once I think you aren't a waste of my time. For now, you are to simply follow my commands, open all doors, stay one step behind me as I walk, and carry any and all things including my purse." her voice was casual. "Inside that refrigerator should be cold beer, I need a glass with a lightly salted rim. Get it for me, on your knees, now." She always thought it was funny watching a nude man walk on his knees carrying something.

He poured some salt onto a plate, wet the rim of a glass and rolled it in the salt like a seasoned bartender. He most intelligently cracked open the beer and left the lid on it, not pouring it into the glass until he made it over to where she was sitting so that he wouldn't spill it while walking on his knees. She watched him intently as he traversed the carpeted hotel room on his knees, his balls and caged cock swinging as he did so with a glass in one hand and the beer in the other. She made note of how he completed the task calmly, efficiently and without mishap. Many times, she has witnessed a green slave, a younger one, be clumsy, rushed, shaking up the beer and making a mess.

He poured the beer into the glass and then handed it to her. She took it from him looking him in the eye as she did.

"Now go and take a shower, on your feet." she had a happy note in her voice " You are to present your body to me clean, always. Inside and out. You will find everything you need inside the restroom. You have 15 minutes." Then he rose to his feet and headed for the restroom to do as he was told. She enjoyed her beer and considered 12. There is something about him. Something she thought she liked.

He reemerged from the restroom with but seconds to spare. He walked across the room toward her and resumed the number two position he had been at before being told to shower.

"How do you feel?" she asked him

"I feel fine" 12 answered.

"Good" She paused for a moment, sipped the beer. "Three" she said and leaving his hands behind his back he leaned back onto his heels bringing his knees almost together. The expression on his face was one of contentment.

She set her beer down on the table and rose to her feet, without a word she disappeared to the restroom leaving him there sitting on his heels. When she returned in only a couple of minutes, she walked up behind him and put a blindfold over his eyes. It was soft, and quite effectively blocked out any light.

"Four" she commanded more loudly this time. He smoothly rose on his knees, bent down and put his nose to the floor. She reached down with her right hand and rubbed his anus with gloved hand. She used a lubed finger, pushing some lube into his opening. Then she put some lube on a large stainless steel butt plug and pushed it into his ass slowly. The shape of the plug was tear dropped and it had a ringed disk with a pink crystal for bling. Once it got to a certain point, the muscles of his sphincter pulled it the rest of the way in. She then wiped away any extra lube from his ass cheeks and said "Five" again being stern and louder. He rose to his knees and spread his legs while putting his hands flat on the carpet. She left the room again with him on all fours. When she returned, he could hear drawers being opened and closed.

What 12 could not see is that she was wearing a very nice black leather, over the bust corset. She had on black lace panties and a smile that might have scared him if he could have seen it. She looked sexy. She looked at herself in the mirror as she stood there. She thought about her perfectly manicured nails and picked up a black leather flogger. It was about two feet long with 24 tails. Seven inches of it was a polished stainless-steel handle that fit nicely in her small hand and came to 2" smooth ball at the end. The metal handle was cool to the touch. She swung it around a few times getting used to its weight. As she did it, she watched in the mirror. Her long, soft hair hanging down around her shoulders.

She walked over and dragged the tails of the flogger over 12 starting at the crack of his plugged and exposed bottom, slowly along his spine up to his head. She stood in front of him, over him, her feet directly in front of his hands. She let the tails of the flogger hang in front of his nose, so that he could smell the leather, then raised it up. She twirled the handle before softly hitting him between the shoulder blades with it. Then, again she brought it down on his back, lower this time. He had not made a sound. She put her right foot on top of his left hand and pushed down as she brought the leather flogger down squarely on his bottom, harder this time. This caused him to exclaim "uhahhh huh!" involuntarily. She repeated the strike, two and then three more times. He was breathing heavy but didn't make another sound.

She removed her foot from his hand and moved to his left side to get a better vantage point of her target. Again, she drug the whip across his back, this time just the tips of the tails, this time from the neck down his spine ending at the pink jewel of the butt plug. Then she brought it down across both of his ass cheeks. Low, where the really tender part is at the top of the thighs. He yelped out of pain and surprise but did not break position. She was quite impressed, actually.

She walked over to the dresser and put the whip inside. "One" she said, and he rose from all fours to position one. She was in front of him, and her long soft hair touched his stomach as she bent down and unlocked the cage around his cock. She stood up straight in front of him and removed the blindfold from his eyes, his face was red from the whipping.

"There are some clothes hanging in the bathroom. Remove your cock cage, and your butt plug. You should clean them both and dry them well. Leave them on the towel atop the toilet tank. You will shower and meet me downstairs at the hotel bar. You have 15 minutes." she said while she rubbed his sore ass. "You did very good, 12. I am proud of you."

He looked her in the eye. There was tension between them that could have been photographed if you had the proper filter lens. "Thank you, my Queen."

She slapped his ass causing him to jump.

He pivoted on the balls of his feet and marched to the restroom like a Solider on the parade field in formation. She watched him walk, slightly off because of the plug in his ass. "On second thought, leave your butt plug in for now, 12" she said after him before he closed the door. "Yes, my Queen, as you wish." then he closed the door. She put some clothes on over the corset, slipped on some shoes and grabbed her purse and headed down to the bar of the hotel.

As instructed he arrived at the bar of the hotel wearing the outfit she had left for him.

He walked over to the table she was sitting alone at. She had a drink in front of her, it was a margarita.

"Please sit down" she said while motioning towards the chair opposite hers. He sat down.

"Tell me, 12, why?" she asked him as she lifted the drink to her lips.

"Why, my Queen?" he was clearly puzzled.

"Yes. Why? Why are you here? I would like to know how you became a slave. How did you get here, with me?"

"Oh." he said. He thought for just a moment, then began "I always thought I knew what I wanted. But I sometimes felt empty. Like there was something I needed to do. I felt sure that people could tell by looking at me that I wasn't where I belonged. I would feel depressed, angry, alone. I grew up on a farm in Kansas. Hard work was what life was about in those days. My father worked like there was no tomorrow. He could not sleep if there was something undone. I left home and attended college in Austin. I loved Texas right away. Even though I dropped out after only two semesters, I stayed. After several jobs in several fields, I landed at an insurance company, and I built my career up until I was in management over auto injury case claims. They transferred me to Reno. Interesting as it was, I felt I was meant for something bigger. More fulfilling."

" What do you drink, 12?" She was flagging over a waitress.

" Jack and coke, please my Queen."

The waitress heard him and when she got to the table kept walking with a grin, repeating " Jack and coke for the big guy!"

" Please continue, 12" Melissa said.

12 took a breath and continued "I happened across some pictures on the internet. I had been looking at porn, but not bdsm or anything. The picture showed a man over a woman's knee, his pants around his ankles. There was a caption that read something like 'A man needs discipline' or something like that. It occurs to me now it was like recruiting poster for the Marines." 12 laughed at himself. The waitress dropped off his drink and another one for Melissa without a word but still had that big grin on her face.

"Anyway, I clicked over to the website, but there wasn't any porn there at all. What was there was a lot of text describing what Femdom and Matriarchy was, the benefits of it, basic protocols and stuff. Phycology of submission and of dominance. That is when I knew what I was. Despite all outward evidence, that was how I felt inside. Reading that changed my life. Over the next couple of years, I read everything I could find on the subject, and there was a lot. One day I saw a website for Femdom Academy." he took a drink of his drink and thought it tasted good. He smiled. "Thank you" he said.

Melissa was literally sitting on the edge of her seat and said, "You earned it.". She smiled.

He went on "There wasn't much information about it. No

pictures. It only said 'Submit. Commit yourself to something of value'. There was an email address, and I wrote an email basically saying who I was, and that I wanted to submit. I received a reply in about 5 minutes asking for my phone number.

I sent all my contact information. Then my phone rang 30 seconds or so after I hit send. The voice on the phone said her name was Mistress Raven and that if I truly wanted the experience of a lifetime, I would need two things. $25,000 cash and all of my affairs in order. If I were to go down this most rewarding path, she could promise me only that if I made it through the program, I would never want to return to my old life and that I would be fulfilled beyond my wildest dreams. She told me the money was only a security deposit to be used for medical needs or burial expenses.

 She said that I only had 48 hours to make up my mind, and if she had not received a call back to the number she called from, I would never be able to contact her again. She also warned me not to tell anyone about it." He stopped to take a drink. He looked around the room, then back at her. She was smiling. She had heard stories about the academy before. But this wasn't the place for one now.

Queen Melissa certainly knew all about the academy. He stopped speaking when she held up her hand in a "stop" motion. She looked at him intently. He had sold himself into slavery, she thought to herself. The rarest of all submissive slaves is the true submissive who not only willing serves a mistress, but one that needed to.

The "Academy", as it was lovingly called, had been started for women to bring their loving, cheating husbands to for reformation. It had dated back to the late nineteenth century or something like that. She wasn't sure.

She suddenly wanted to be back in the room with him. She suggested they take their drinks back upstairs. Along the way back to the room she saw their reflection in a window, and she could see he was smiling as he walked behind her, carrying both of their drinks, as well as her purse. She could see that he also saw that she was smiling too.

At the door she opened the door and stood aside as he entered. "Set those down over on the table" and she excused herself into the restroom without a word.

When she came out, she had removed her clothing to again having nothing on other than the corset and black lace panties. He, however, was still dressed. Standing near the table.

"Strip!" she shouted. "While in this room you will not cover yourself." she said angrily. "This will be the same when we get home, or wherever we are unless I tell you otherwise!"

He quickly did as she asked and placed the clothes in the same drawer his other clothes were in. Now nude he turned to see that she had produced a heavy leather paddle.

"PUT YOUR HANDS ON THE CHAIR!" she said loudly. He did what he was told and as soon as his hands touched the seat of the chair the first blow struck him. Thwack. He felt it. Two more followed in quick succession. Thwack. Thwack. He was just about to catch his breath when the third and fourth then fifth came just as quickly. Thwack, Thwack, Thwack. He tried not to move, not to break position but he was unable to stand and sank almost to his knees from the sharp pain. She stopped and he resumed his position.

"Breath" she said. Then hit him again. Thwack.

" How will you address me?" she asked

" My Queen" he answered

" What is your attire at home to be?"

" Nude unless otherwise instructed, my Queen." his voice was shaking.

"One" she commanded, and he stood up but didn't turn to face her. He spread his legs and put his hands on his head. She grabbed his balls in her right hand, still holding the paddle in her left one.

"Who do these belong to?" she asked looking at his cock grow.

"They belong to you, my Queen."

"Very good." She held on to his balls a minute longer, gave them a squeeze and let them go. She walked around him, rubbed his now sore ass on both cheeks and sat down in the chair.

"Twelve, turn to face me. Always turn to face me unless I tell you otherwise to hold or to stay. But I will say hold, you are not a dog after all, are you? ARE YOU A DOG?! ANSWER ME!!!" again her confident voice cracked as she screamed at him.

"No, my Queen"

"Good" she said. "I don't need a dog. I need a man, but with a dog's obedience and loyalty. But a man." She smiled as she looked at him. "You are certainly not a dog. Two." and she pointed to a spot at her feet. He took position there. She sat in the chair and looked at him for a few minutes. "Take your hands off of your head and relax your arms. I want to watch you give me a show. Stroke yourself. But do not orgasm. If you cum without my permission, I will have to punish you. Is that understood?"

"Yes, my Queen" and he began stroking his now hard cock. She lifted her left foot and put it on his face while she watched. He began to kiss the soles of her feet. She moved her foot to get the toes into his mouth and delighted at the sight of him masturbating. He had a nice cock. He was circumcised, about seven and a half inches she guessed, maybe eight. He sucked her toes. She was enjoying it. His tongue was magic. He reached up to support her leg just above the ankle. He moved her leg for access to her heel and arch while gently massaging her calf, all the while slowly stroking himself. She let this go on before switching feet. She was so aroused. His strokes became even slower. She reached her drink on the table and sipped it while enjoying this foot worship.

"12, I want you to go to the restroom and remove your butt plug now. Clean it and dry it. Place it next to your chastity cage. Then return here after you have cleaned yourself as well. I plan to fuck you."

When he returned from the restroom, he could see she was now wearing a harness and large dildo. "That is going to be too large, I think." 12 said. The smile left her face. She grabbed the black lace panties from the floor and walked over to him.

"Open your mouth. "She demanded. He did so and she slowly

stuffed the panties into his mouth. "If I want your opinion, I will ask you for it. How dare YOU tell me something? It is of very little concern to me. I didn't tell you to think. SO DON'T DO IT!!!" Her voice cracked at the end, and it scared him a bit. Then he felt the pain as she grabbed his testicles in her hand again, hard, and pulled while squeezing them. He moaned with pain, but she pulled harder. "Get on your knees, 12" she said softly, letting go of his balls. She noticed how hard he was now.

As he got down on his knees, she removed her panties from his mouth. She walked over to a table and picked up a bottle of water. He watched her walk with the large dildo bobbing in front of her. She returned to where he was on his knees and opened the bottle of water. "Open your mouth" and he did so. She grabbed his hair and pulled his head back and poured some of the water in his mouth. He swallowed all that he could but quite a bit of it spilled out. She set the bottle down on the floor. She positioned herself in front of him and held the dildo in her right hand, his hair in her left pulled his mouth to the tip of the rubber cock. She slowly pushed it into his mouth until all of the head was in. She stopped. "I want you to suck it." She said. He did. She watched him suck just the head of her strap on cock for a minute or so, then she pulled away from him, letting go of his hair. "Come here" she said pointing to the bed. "Bend over the bed, legs spread." He got up and did as she asked, hands still behind his back. She applied some lube to his ass and to her rubber cock, stroking its length. She put the head of it to his ass and pushed in slowly, but completely until it was all inside of him. His breathing was now in deep breaths. She stopped, completely filling him, allowing his adjustment. After a minute or so she pulled back an inch or so then thrust back into him violently. He gasped as he saw stars. The base of the dong hit her just right against her clit, and the pleasure ran thru her. She did the same thing, pulling back an inch slowly then rammed the rubber dick back into him as hard as she could thrust. She did it a few times more like that before pulling back further and further, each time slamming back into him causing him to gasp and breath in sharply. Then she picked up the pace, each thrust into his ass bringing her closer to her orgasm which came soon causing her to lean over his back. She did not stop. She grabbed onto his wrists and used his arms to pull her dick into him. She fucked him feverishly until she orgasmed another two times before stopping.

She pulled the dildo out of him and stepped back from him. She could see a stream of precum leaking from his cock, but he had no erection. Leaving him in the position, and without removing the strap on, she walked over to the dresser and grabbed the flogger again. She let his ass have several hard whacks with the flogger. One of her strikes had hit his testicles and it caused him to yelp. His cock was hard now. She put some more lube on her cock, setting the flogger next to his face on the bed, grabbed his wrists again and began fucking him some more. He was sighing when she had one more orgasm and stopped. She pulled out of him again and removed the strap on and harness. She went into the restroom and put it in the sink. She poured a glass of beer and sat in the upholstered chair. Her sex was wet and hot from her orgasms. "Come over here, 12, and clean me with your tongue." He raised from the bed and crawled over to her placing his mouth on her swollen clit and began licking and sucking her juice. She drank her beer while he serviced her, but she was no longer aroused. "That is enough, thank you, 12." He stopped then backed away from her, his face wet with her juice. "Go clean yourself up in the restroom, 12. Clean and store my big cock and harness."

Upon his return to the room, he found her in the bed under the covers, sleeping. There was a pallet made of blankets and a single pillow on the floor at the foot of the bed. He stored the strap on in the drawer, there were many other sex toys in that drawer he could see, but he did not spend a second examining them. He was no snoop, he thought. He laid down and covered up falling asleep quickly. Smiling.

He awoke and she was still sleeping. After using the restroom, he brushed his teeth, washed his face, shaved his face and combed his hair. Having no directive on what he was to do now, he decided not to wake her, but to dress and go downstairs for breakfast. He had scrambled eggs, sausage and some toasted wheat bread buttered. Drank a cup of coffee. He had a tray made for his Queen and brought it for her back to the room. She woke up when he came back into the room. She saw he had the tray and asked, "what is that?" she sat up covering up her naked breast with the sheet as she asked.

"Breakfast for you, my Queen."

"Oh, thank you, 12."

He brought the tray over to the bed and removed the cover from the plate revealing the meal of scrambled eggs, sausage, bacon, hash browns, toast buttered. There was also a glass of orange juice and a cup of coffee.

"Oh my, that is way too much!" she said taking the tray. He stepped away and began taking off his clothes as she ate, watching him. He stood at the number one position with his hands on top of his head, legs spread, facing her.

"Relax your arms." She said to him in between bites. She took another bite and a sip of the orange juice before saying "I need to use the restroom" And she set the tray on the bed and walked to the restroom, nude. He enjoyed the sight of her, and it showed on his face. She smiled back at him. She returned, still nude, after ten minutes. She had clearly showered. She walked up behind him and put her arms around him from behind, reaching around to his chest. She pinched both of his nipples and laid her cheek against his shoulder blade. He began to get an erection, which she noticed when her hand made its way down his not quite flat stomach to his cock. She gently held his growing erection in her left hand, her right hand still playing with his nipple. She kissed his back and stepped away from him, leaving him with a now very hard cock. She climbed back into bed and picked up her breakfast tray and said, "Take this, 12." as she lifted up the tray to him. He immediately stepped over and took the tray from her. Took it over to the room door, opening the door slowly to see if anyone was in the hall. Seeing that no one was outside the room he stepped partly thru the door and set the tray down on the floor outside left of the door. He returned to the place he stood but before he got there, she pulled the covers back and told him "Come over here and get your tongue busy, 12." She pointed at her pussy. She laid back onto the pillows as he crawled between her raised legs and began to softly lick her outer labia. He gently sucked the lips into his mouth. She tasted sweet, and salty. He loved her taste, her smell, her essence. He licked slowly, steadily, along both sides before softly running his tongue at her center from the bottom to the top a couple times. He darted his tongue inside her opening, and she moaned so he did it again and again. She loved how he did this.

Just then the phone to the hotel room softly rang. "Don't stop, 12 it's okay, just keep doing. Exactly. That." And then she reached over and answered the phone. "Hello." She said in a very normal voice. "Yes, this is her. 2:30? Okay that would be fine. Thank you." And she hung up the phone. "You are really doing a nice job, 12. You are very skilled. That call was a little surprise I have arranged." She smiled devilishly "I know you are going to like it."

He continued servicing her pussy for another 20 maybe 30 minutes, he lost track of time. His tongue and his neck were both quite soar, but his cock was quite hard. When she had enough, she said "okay, that's enough for now, 12. You can get up and stand over there" she was pointing at the corner near the window. "Facing the corner" she added coolly.

As he stood in the corner, he could hear her moving about the room doing things. There was a knock on the room door, and she went over to answer the knock. Opening the door, he heard her say "Oh good. Right on time. Come right in." her voice cheerful and sweet. He wanted to turn and see what was happening but thought better of it. But not too long after whoever it was had arrived, seen the naked man standing by the window, they had left without so much as a word. He heard her say "Thank you. ", in the same cheerful way she had greeted them as she closed the door behind them.

Melissa walked up behind 12 and put her hands on his back, then she kissed his back between his shoulder blades. He loved the way she touched him, feeling her skin on his. The way her hair felt as she moved her hands around him and put her cheek on his back in the same spot, she kissed him. She rubbed his biceps, and her warmth was very nice. They breathed together for a few moments, and it felt good to both of them. She liked the way he reacted to her touch, even after her whipping him. Some men don't react so well. 12 was something special, she thought.

She lowered her right hand down to his cock, and it was starting to get hard. She just liked feeling it in her hand. She felt powerful being able to grab a man anytime she wanted. Make them think and feel what she wanted them to. She knew at a young age that she had power over men. This one is no different than any of them. Well, maybe he is different, she thought. He certainly made her feel different. She continued to fondle him, feel him get completely hard in her hand. She used her left hand to explore his body, running it from his nipple down to his ass. She caressed his firm ass cheek, grabbing it and squeezing it from the underside. He moaned as she let go of him and stepped away but did not turn his head. He continued to look straight ahead. She returned moments later and put the blind fold back over his eyes completely blinding him. She reached back around him and grabbed his still hard cock in her hand and pulled him with it. She directed him over to the bed and then with her other hand pushed him in the center of his chest while pulling his cock until he was sitting on the edge of the bed. She pumped his cock a couple of more times, then removed her hand. He sat there like that for what felt to him like an hour. His cock started to soften. He could hear her moving around the room doing things again. It sounded to him like she was dressing. He wondered to himself what was about to happen.

"What do you want, 12?" she asked in a sweet soft voice, almost seductive. "I want to serve you, my Queen." He answered. "Why, 12, why do you want to serve me?" He thought for a moment before answering. "Because I belong to you. You deserve to be happy, and it would make me happy to make you happy." He could feel her close now, in front of him. "And?" she asked now on her knees in front of him. "Why is that 12?" she asked him as she again took hold of his soft, but now hardening cock and cupped his balls with her other hand, softly massaging them. He moaned then began "I feel that you deserve for me to please you in every way possible." She stroked him and as she did, he became very hard in her hand. "Go on, 12. Tell me all about why you want to serve me." As she said that she bent down and took the head of his cock in her mouth. She licked him all around his glans in a circular motion before taking half of him in her mouth. Her hand rose up to his chest and she played with his nipples before pushing him back. He supported himself with his elbows wishing he could see her doing this to him. She moved her head very slowly up and down, only about an inch or so, taking him into her mouth deeper each time. "I live to serve. To submit. I am lucky to be owned by you, such a beautiful, wonderful woman. I wish to keep you happy so that you will keep me. I am so happy being yours!" His breathing was faster now, and he feared he would cum any second. She stopped and pulled her head all the way up, his cock fell onto his stomach. Her hands were on both of his thighs, gripping them. She moved down and sucked one of his testicles into her mouth, then the other. She licked his scrotum and then all the way up the bottom side of his cock, stopping at the head of his cock she flicked the underside over and over with her tongue. Then she stopped, raised her head and got up. He moaned out of frustration. She truly had him on the edge. He was on the verge of release. He remained laying back on his elbows, his swollen cock throbbing on its own.

"I see you are in a state" she said in a 'as a matter of fact' tone. "I suppose you want me to make *you* cum?" Melissa looked at him, took him in. She examined him, liking what she saw. The fact that she did not select him made this somehow more exciting for her. It is true that she would not have bid on a slave this old, or in his less than perfect physical appearance.   But his skill with his tongue, the sound of his voice and the way she felt so comfortable with him made her shiver. He had shown her he was fairly well trained, certainly trainable anyway. He had taken her flogger very well. His masculinity still very intact even after she fucked his ass with a strap on.

"12, I want you to get up and take off that blindfold." He rose quickly to his feet pulling the blindfold from his eyes and off his head. He stood there at the foot of the bed at the number one position, legs spread and hands on his head still holding the blindfold. His eyes struggling with the light. His cock still quite hard. His breath still short.

As she looked at him for a moment she thought about his cock, and it made her want him. As a rule, she rarely ever allowed a man to penetrate her. She was surprised she had those thoughts. It had been a long time. Over a year she thought.

As he stood there, he saw that she was dressed. She was wearing a royal blue blouse that had sleeves just past her elbow and black lace almost to her wrist. It had a high neckline but was cut in the center about 5 inches down between her breasts. She was wearing black baggy pants and leather boots that had a slight heel and a pointy toe. He also noticed that luggage had been delivered and placed near the door.

"We are going home, 12" she told him smiling. "I want you to shower, put on your cage, and fix yourself up nice. There are some clothes for you hanging on the bathroom door." She held up the key to his cock cage on the leather tag for him to see "I have your key." She smiled at him. "I am going down to the bar. Meet me there whenever you are finished packing everything and have the bags downstairs." With that she turned and walked out the door. He looked down at his suffering erection, thought about masturbating, then decided not to. He would ride this wave of frustration, not wanting to spoil anything that may come. He did as she asked, showered, and put on his chastity cage. Locked it. The clothes she left for him was a black suit and dress shoes. The shirt was crisp and white. There was not a tie, so he left 2 buttons undone. It took about an hour to pack the room into the 6 suitcases. While he was packing, he had a chance to inspect the contents of the drawer that held her paddle and her flogger. There were quite a few other things in there, some of which he wasn't sure about their intended purpose, but he felt the pressure on his cock cage as his arousal was evident. He smiled.

He loaded the bags onto a gondola he found in the hallway outside the room. He looked at himself in the mirror and he thought he looked pretty sharp. He was sure that she would be pleased, and he wondered about where they were going. He knew better than to ask. After bringing the gondola down the elevator he parked it between the reception desk and the entrance to the bar. He could see her. She was sitting alone having a drink and she waved him over. He liked her smile, he thought as he headed over there. "You look nice." She said motioning for him to sit. "You took longer than I expected you to, we will talk more about that later." Her smile faded to a half smile, and she looked at him quite sternly. "I am quite demanding at times, 12, do you think you are up for the challenge?". He did not hesitate to answer "Yes, my Queen. I desire to serve you to your satisfaction." He knew it was true as soon as he said it. He felt delighted to be serving her, and he would try even harder than he was trying now if that is what she required. Being hers is everything he could imagine wanting at this moment or ever again, for that matter. "I am sorry I failed you, my Queen." She looked at his face and could see the sudden question confused him. "I am sure you will be, 12." She looked at him sitting across the table. He did look very handsome. "I think we will continue to get along well, 12. If we do, there will not be an issue. But know this. I do not tolerate brats. If you do become a brat suddenly, I will be done with you, and you will go back to the auction house. Are we very clear about that?" he again did not hesitate to answer her while keeping eye contact with her very beautiful and expressive eyes "Yes, my Queen. Very clear."

"Good. That understanding out of the way I want to explain what I expect from you. But do not think that I may not demand something different or change at any time.....anything. but to start with, as you are intelligent, handsome, well-spoken and mature, you are to be my service slave. You will be replacing a younger slave who served me for only about a year before she developed emotional problems. It happens sometimes, can't be helped. I let her go, and she has left the life." She sipped her drink, then continued "I have been managing well without her for almost a year now, but now that you have fell into my lap I may as well make use of you. I do intend on making use of you, 12. I want you to know that." He looked at her and she wasn't smiling. He thought that she looked happy though. Her eyes were smiling. She continued "I keep a domestic slave year-round who cooks and cleans, or whatever I require of her. Then I have 2 slaves I loan to another owner. In the spring they are with me until the fall. They primarily keep the grounds, maintain the pool, or whatever I require. So, your duties will be whatever I need of you, also. You will be my personal assistant, you will be my groomer, you will be a butler, you will be a driver when I want one. You will be my foot stool or my ashtray if I tell you to. One other thing.... you will answer to all the other slaves in the house. You are on the bottom. I want that clear right now. Any of my other slaves have full authority over you. If you can accept this, you might fit in. Somehow." She took another sip of her drink. "What do you think, 12?" she asked softly. He quickly responded, "I will serve to please you, my Queen." He meant what he said, but he was nervous. He really never considered that situation. "I expect you to, 12. Okay. Let's go home. I drove the truck here; it should be waiting outside. Load the bags and get the heater warmed up, I will be there shortly." She smiled and he got up and said, "Yes my Queen." She handed him a gold key chain with a single key on it and a gold fob that had an engraved crown on one side of it. He bowed and turned and walked back to the gondola. Pushing it out the door he saw her truck. There was no way to confuse this truck with someone else's. This truck belonged to a Queen. It was pearl white with dark tint windows, crew cab dually, and the center caps on the gold wheels had the same crown that the fob had on it.

"Say it again" Melissa said as she stood in front of 12 with her right foot on his left hand. Her hair was held back into a ponytail. She was wearing a pair of white jogging shorts and a tight-fitting white tee shirt that really showed off her curves. She held a riding crop in both hands. 12 was on his knees with his elbows on the hardwood floor of her office, his hands also flat on the floor. He felt exquisitely submissive to this powerful, beautiful woman. He had given up everything, walked away from his life, to find exactly this. He felt very lucky.

"I am going to be more submissive today.
I will be respectful and obedient.
I understand that I must obey my Queen.
I succeed in life, because I obey my Queen.
I will demonstrate my obedience and give thanks every day.
Thank you, my Queen, for your dominance." He answered, getting it right for the first time. He breathed a sigh of relief realizing that he got it right even before she said "Very good, 12. Very, very good. I was beginning to wonder if you could do it." Melissa enjoyed having 12 at the ranch. She was growing fond of him. He made her happy. She especially liked his oral abilities. His ability to take abuse was above average. She also found him to be attractive. She still had not allowed him to penetrate her, but she had penetrated him on a regular basis. She wanted his cock though, so she would have it soon enough. When she was ready.

She raised her foot off of his hand and stepped to his side to inspect his ass. She had marked him up with the riding crop. But not too bad. Still though, his tears were real. She bent over him and setting the crop down on his back she ran her hands over his wombs, gently soothing him. "Okay, up with you. On your feet." And as she stepped away taking the evil instrument of pain, she had just played a symphony on his ass with, he rose to his feet. His tears were indeed real. He had not been whipped like that before. Still though, he was able to take that punishment. He actually enjoyed a lot of it, and he was proud that he did not use his safe word. It made him proud to endure as much as he could, to push himself. For her.

Queen Melissa never took things too far, also, she always cared for him so well afterwards. He had been with her at the ranch for almost a month now and he was still adapting to his life. Being Melissa's service slave, or her personal slave as he thought of it, was indeed challenging sometimes. Equally rewarding in many ways. It was only Melissa and another slave, Gretchen, at the house right now. Gretchen did most of the cooking and cleaning. Gretchen was a German woman who stood almost 7 feet tall. She was larger than life. She had huge muscles, very lean, very tone. She had been an Olympic body builder once upon a time. She wore tight spandex shorts and a jogging bra under her apron nearly always. Her breasts were large, but not in proportion to her body. She was both sexy and terrifying at the same time. She was also a marvelous chef, cooking very elaborate and healthy meals from scratch. Her feet were crazy big. She wore ballet slippers most of the time. Those had to be custom made, he thought. She would kill him if she could hear his thoughts. Gretchen could literally squash 12 like a bug. He worked for Gretchen most every morning. She was indifferent to him, neither friendly nor adversarial. He was pretty sure she did not have a since of humor, or at least he had never heard her laugh. He had seen her smile a few times though. Sometimes she would whistle or hum while she went through her task. She made everything she did seem effortless. Her work was not labor to her. She just did it, not ever getting tired or even sweating. She was pleasant, overall. She would tell him what to do, show him how it was to be done, and he did it. When he was in the kitchen, he was to always wear an apron. But at all other times he was to remain nude. Gretchen seemed oblivious to his nudeness neither commenting nor even noticing other than to tell him to put on an apron to cover himself.

Melissa wiped his tears with her thumbs. "I want you to remember your Mantra, and I want you to say it to yourself in the mirror each morning." She ran her hands down the front of his chest until both of her hands held his caged cock and his balls. "Also, whenever I ask you." She looked him in the eye. He thought this felt nice. She attached a leash to the lock on his chastity cage and said "Heel." And began walking towards the door. He of course followed being led by his cock cage. She opened the door and headed for the kitchen with 12 in tow. Once in the kitchen Gretchen noticed the situation but said nothing. "Gretchen, I need some cream for poor 12's bottom. Do we have any?". Gretchen turned to face her and answered "Of course, my Queen." With a smile, then turned and walked to the pantry, which was a huge room lined with shelves and three rows of shelves in the middle jammed full of every kind of product you could imagine. She returned with a jar of salve and handed it to Melissa. "Thank you my dear" Melissa said, taking the jar. Gretchen leaned down and Melissa gave her a kiss on the lips. She then turned and headed out the back door, 12 in tow. The back patio was very nice. There was a table and chairs, a porch swing and some potted plants of many varieties. There was an enormous propane grill with a cover on it. Down two steps was the pool deck. The pool was quite large as well. To the right of the pool there was a large tree. It had a rope hanging from a branch with a hook on the end. At the top it went thru a pulley that was strapped to a large branch, and back down to the trunk of the tree. There it was wrapped around a cleat bolted to the tree. It had been there for a while as the bark was growing around it. She led him down to the tree and stopped him under the hook. "Open your mouth" she said. He did as he was told and then she put the handle of the leash in his mouth. He understood what she wanted, so he closed his mouth holding the leash between his teeth. The wind was a little chilly, it was March, and the sun was bright, the sky was blue. It was in the 70's but still there was a chill in the air. His naked flesh goose bumped all over. He could feel it on his legs, up both arms. She walked over and released the rope from the cleat and lowered the hook. She walked back over and took the handle from his mouth. She bent down and brought the leash between his legs and up between his ass cheeks. The chain felt cold. She then put the leather loop of the handle on the hook. Walking back over to the tree she pulled the rope, and it pulled his chastity cage back and the chain was taunt. He could still stand flat on his feet, but it caused discomfort. If he raised on one or both feet, he was fine. It caused him to do a sort of dance between feet as she secured the rope. She opened the jar and spread the salve over his ass cheeks, which by now he had completely forgotten about. But that did feel nice. She cooed as she did it. "Poor baby" she said. "Okay. All better!" and he continued to dance from foot to foot. He tried to shift the cage using his hands to zero success. Melissa started laughing. "Oh my. I suppose the rope is too high. Let me get you some slack. I am not trying to hang you by your balls. Although....... Just kidding!" And she walked over and loosened the rope. He was very relieved. Then without a word she walked back into the house. He rubbed his cage where it had pulled against him. He stood there, not able to take more than one step in any direction, for what felt like hours. Finally, the back door opened, and Gretchen came out. Thank God, 12 thought. She had a bag in her hand. She looked at 12 and shook her head but did not say a word. She picked up a table, a rather large table made of expanded metal, in one hand and carried it down near where 12 was standing, unable to move. Setting the table down she put the bag on top of it and opened the bag. From the bag she produced two leather wrist cuffs. The cuffs were black with furry padding on the inner surface. She walked over to 12 and politely said "Put out your arms now, please 12" looking at him thoughtfully. He did as she asked. She put the cuffs on his wrist. "Thank you, Gretchen." 12 said softly. Gretchen reached down between his legs and released the leash from the lock on his cock cage. "You're welcome, 12." She said mockingly in a similar soft voice. She reached up and removed the leash from the hook with very little effort, it was well in her reach. She walked back over to where the bag was on the table. From the bag she pulled out some chain. It had a latching hook on both ends, he could see, as she brought it over and hooked one end on his right cuff and the other on the hook that dangled from the tree. His right arm was now over his head, but not very high. He could bend his arm somewhat. His left arm was free. He had no idea what was going to happen. Gretchen had never punished him or played with him before. He had only ever seen her work. "What's going on Gretchen?" 12 asked softly again. "What are you going to do to me?"

She thought about answering him. What could she say to him? She decided to try. "It is best if you don't know. More fun if it is a surprise. Don't worry, 12. You will be okay. Now be quite!" and she pinched his nipple. She smiled at him as she walked over to another tree. It had a cleat on it too. He was surprised he had not seen it while he stood there. He had been focused on the house, trying to see if anyone was coming back. She lowered another hook from another branch. Going back to her bag, she produced another chain. She walked with authority back over to him and took his left arm and fastened the hook to the cuff. Taking the chain over to the other hook that was now dangling from another branch. When she pulled that rope taunt it stretched his arms to the maximum without lifting him from the ground but making movement impossible. She checked the tension of both ropes and the cuffs on his wrist for proper fitment. When she was satisfied with the situation she again went back to the bag. She produced a blindfold. She put it on his eyes and blocked out his vision. She kissed him lightly on the lips. That shocked him completely.

The hot wax was applied with a special brush, and immediately Gretchen pressed on the wide cloth strips. The first one that she pulled off of 12's chest caused him to yell out in pain. He had no idea what was going on until now.

"Scream, scream, 12. It's okay. On these 99 acres there is no one to hear you but yourself. You would be wise to remember that if you have the urge to resist me, that knowledge may keep you from making some sort of…." She paused while she pulled another one off causing 12 to scream out again. "…. mistake. I don't relish causing you pain, 12. But I also don't mind it either. Okay?" his eyes were full of tears. She grew tired of waiting for an answer he wasn't giving, so she took his balls in her very large hand and squeezed causing him to see nothing but white even though he had a blindfold on. "Okay?" she asked again very softly. She had power in her hands. He thought she was ripping his balls off. He had had his balls squeezed, slapped, even kicked and whipped but Gretchen and her master race grip was more painful than anything he had ever felt. "Okay. Okay. Okay. Ah Christ please! Okay!" he blurted almost in one syllable. She let go. "Good. I am glad that we have that all cleared up. So just scream if you need to, but do not fight me. Our Queen wants you completely free of your body hair. So. You will be completely free of it." She said it in her heavy German accent, while applying more wax to more hair and putting on more strips. "Why?" He asked. That obviously amused her, she laughed for the first time that he had ever heard her laugh. Then she pulled the strip of wax and hair off of him. "You ought to do yourself a favor right now, 12. Stop wondering about why so much. It doesn't matter the why. She wants you smooth, smooth you will be." And she pulled another strip off, and then another right after. "Be still. If you keep wiggling this takes too long, and I get frustrated with you." He tried to be as still as he could. She started to whistle just like she did while mopping or dusting. Steady putting on the wax and ripping his hair out by the root. When his chest, arms, armpits and back were completely hairless, she stopped. Walking over to the table she rummaged in the bag until she found what she looked for and came back to 12. She looked at him there, bound by his arms, hairless from the waist up and obviously in pain from the abusive waxing. She went back to the table and grabbed a can of lidocaine aloe spray, the type used on sunburns. Taking mercy on him she sprayed the areas she had previously attacked. The spray was so cold he didn't know if he could take it either but quickly, he was pain free and didn't care about being cold. One thing for sure is he had surely forgotten all about the marks on his ass from Melissa's riding crop. He didn't even feel it anymore. Realizing that, he felt prideful. He could endure this with more dignity, he thought. He promised himself he would. He raised his chin and faced the sky that he could not see.

Gretchen unlocked his chastity cage causing 12 to again be startled. He had not been unlocked at all in almost a month since they left the hotel in Waco. As she removed the stainless-steel cage from his cock it sprang to life quickly becoming erect. She removed the base ring from around his scrotum and cock. She saw his erecting cock and thought to herself that, although she had seen much larger, 12 was of a nice size. He ached to touch himself. To stroke his cock. To rub it and his very blue balls. She went over to the table and set down the chastity device, grabbed a damp cloth, and proceeded to wipe his genitals down. She lingered some, enjoying the sounds of pleasure and relief he made. Using a dry cloth, she dried him off. Then she was back to business waxing off all of his pubic hair as well. She worked in a steady, slow methodical method, being very mindful to not miss a single hair. Both of his legs, which she had him raise and rest on her shoulders, the crack of his ass down to his feet. She even removed the hair from his toes. Inspecting him thoroughly and using tweezers to pluck any hairs that she missed. Then she sprayed his lower body with the lidocaine spay, and she took the time to rub it in. He had an erection before she got to his cock. Taking his cock in her giant hand, pumping him slowly, he felt tiny. Small. Insignificant. He had not expected that, and he came close to cumming. Denied an orgasm, she stopped and let go of his penis. "tisk, tisk." She said. "Naughty boy."

She released the rope to his right hand, then to his left. She removed the cuffs and waxed smooth his wrist and hands. One at a time. She removed his blind fold. It was nearly dark now, but he still needed a minute to adjust his eyes. Before his eyes adjusted Gretchen had taken his hands and locked steel hand cuffs on both wrist in front of his hairless torso. To the chain that connected the cuffs together she attached a leash without a word. Walking towards the house she pulled him along with the leash. He was led through a quiet part of the house to a part of it he had not been before and entering a room he assumed was her quarters. It was large, nicely furnished, very orderly. There was a sofa in part of the room that faced a window overlooking a pasture. He could see an old stable with a rusty roof. Between the window and the corner was a tall armoire. It was plain cherry wood but had ornate hinges and door pulls made of tarnished brass. The bed was a king size bed made up very smartly with a sea foam green blanket. Inside the spacious room the door to her private bathroom was open and the light was on inside. She pulled him along to the bathroom, after closing the door to her room behind them. Stopping outside the bathroom she pointed to the floor, giving a hand signal, that of which he understood, but had not seen since the academy. Not everyone used hand signals, but it is taught to everyone in the academy. The signal she made was her index finger and forefinger separated and pointing down. It meant kneel with your legs spread. That is what he did. She dangled the handle of his leash in front of his mouth. He knew what she wanted again and opened his mouth to take the handle between his teeth. Without a word she went into the bathroom and closed the door. He could hear the water running in the tub, and after a few minutes Gretchen opened the door. She was totally nude. Her nipples were larger around than his thumbs were and very red. Her areolas were silver dollar size, not small, but on her large breast they looked small. She was well built, and he had not really appreciated how sexy she was before this moment. His cock started to get hard, again. She reached out and took the handle of the leash from his mouth and she wrapped the leash around her hand choking up on it until she had the chain of the handcuffs an inch from his hand. She turned and dragged him five or so feet into the bathroom with him trying to move his legs on his knees frantically trying to keep up. She turned, reached down, and picked the grown man up into her arms like a small child tight against her breast and stepped into the large tub with him. She let go of his legs once she sat down and pulled his back against her. She grabbed a large sponge and soaped it up with some nice smelling liquid soap. She then began to bath him, rubbing the soap all along his body. He relaxed so much he almost fell asleep. He could not believe this was happening. She washed the hair on his head, then she conditioned it. She moved him where she wanted him without any words and washed him between the legs paying some attention to his anus. She then turned him to face her, and she washed herself, head to toe. When she finished, she pulled the lever starting to drain the tub then stood up. She offered him a hand to stand up, and he took it, finding it to be very sturdy, steady and helpful. They both stepped out as she grabbed a towel and put it around his shoulders, and then grabbed another one and she dried herself off. She produced a key and unlocked then removed his handcuffs, rubbing his wrist as she looked him in the eye. She handed him a bottle of baby oil and he began to rub it in to her skin. He didn't miss an inch. He went over and over some areas. Very impressed with the way her muscles felt under her skin. Her breast were firm and somehow also very soft. Her vagina was almost completely devoid of hair. There was a very small landing strip patch, about an inch wide and maybe two inches long, right above her large clit. Her labia was not very big. Like her nipples, it wasn't small, but not in proportion to the rest of her. She was very pink between her lips, and he wished to lean in and taste her. She was a marvelous woman. She then took the baby oil and rubbed his hairless body completely with it. He tried to put his arms around her. But then she stopped him and said "That was nice. Now we know each other better. You may leave to your quarters. I will see you in the morning at 6am. We have a big day tomorrow. Get some rest." And she bent down and gave him a peck on the lips reached around and gave him a pinch on his hairless butt. He turned and left her room.

She closed the door behind him. It was a big day today, in his opinion. Gretchen made him feel very small and also very protected. He felt strange being free of all body hair. When he got into his bed, pulled the sheet over his body, he could feel everything. The odor from the baby oil filled his nose. It aroused him. His cock was hard. He ran his hands over his hairless balls, smooth and sensitive. The sensations were new and different. He forced himself to stop touching himself. He really was quite tired, and he did not want a punishment for masturbating. So, then he rolled onto his side and fell asleep.

12's normal morning routine was to make himself clean, inside and out, by showering. There was a nozzle attached to a long hose in his shower he was to use to achieve this. His alarm woke him every morning at five, and he was to report to Gretchen in the kitchen to begin his day, doing whatever she needed. As most everyday she did not need or perhaps want his help with breakfast, she would assign him a cleaning task he was to perform. After breakfast was ready Gretchen had him eat breakfast with her. Then he would bring Queen Melissa her breakfast in bed. After that Melissa, took charge of him. She was training him to serve her how she wanted to be served. He really quite enjoyed it. He loved her. No two ways about it. He had fallen in love with his Queen.

Today was different. At four thirty before his alarm went off, he was awakened by Gretchen pulling his covers off of him. She stood over him and he could see through his not quite open eyes that she was dressed differently, and she was holding a glass of something. "Wake up." She said in a normal voice. "You need to drink this." Gretchen held the drink forward to him. 12 sat up on his arms and then with his left hand reached up to grab the glass. He wondered what it was. He looked at the white liquid in the glass, then up at her. He was about to ask her what it was, why he needed to drink it, what time was it, and about a hundred other questions when she said "don't talk. Drink it now." And he thought better of trying her patience. He didn't know what the crap was that he was drinking, but he knew it was horrible. It tasted like chalk, with a hint of limestone. The odor reminded him of vitamin store. He compliantly drank all of it, struggling to keep it down. "Okay. Now get up, on your feet and turn around with your back to me." He did what she commanded. "Put your hands on your head." As soon as he did, she grabbed his right hand and expertly pulled it behind him and put a handcuff on his wrist in one motion and then pulled his left and did the same thing. She would have been an excellent cop, he thought to himself. This was a different pair of handcuffs. The chain that linked them together was much shorter. He wondered if she might be angry, but she wasn't acting angry, so he let that go. She put her hand on the back of his neck and turned him pushing him towards the door. He started to get scared and because he didn't know what was happening, he resisted slightly. Her giant hand squeezed his neck and he stopped resisting. She took him down the hallway towards a side door to the outside. It was still very dark, and it was cold. His hairless body was shivering as they proceeded down a path towards the old stable. He had not been there yet, but he was fairly certain there weren't any horses in there. The dirt was moist under his feet and came up between his toes. Whatever he had drank was churning inside his stomach and he felt sick. She was almost lifting him by his neck as she pushed him down the path. The stable was easily a hundred yards from the house. He could see that there was a light on inside. His shivering made his nausea worse. When he started heaving, she stopped, and he bent over at the waist and puked. He puked so much it scared him. She didn't seem pleased or surprised either. When he stood up straight again, she put her hand on his neck again, softer this time, and they continued down the path. Reaching the stable he could feel the warmth coming from inside even before she opened a door and pushed him gently through it. It wasn't a stable at all. The floors were tiled with large, green ceramic tiles. There were several floor drains throughout the room and the tiles were cut and sloped in a very intricate way draining to them. The rafters were made of red iron and a low I beam ran the length of the room. There was a support beam rising up from the floor holding its weight. He could see there was duct work and an air handler suspended above the beam. The lighting came from large commercial fixtures he had seen before inside a big box store or something. Obviously, Queen Melissa had this built with the exterior made to look like an old horse stable, camouflaging what was really a state of the art, fully equipped dungeon.

Gretchen stopped him and grabbed a hose by the door and proceeded to hose him off from the waist down, getting the mud off his feet and the puke splatter off of his legs. She hosed herself off too. She reached behind him and unlocked his cuffs. Leaving him standing where he was, she walked to the corner to the right of the door where there was a kitchenette. Opening a refrigerator, she got out a couple of bottles of water. "Come on, drink this." She said motioning for him to come to her. He moved towards her and noticed that the tile floors had some type of non-slip coating on them. He took the water and drank it completely, then took the other one and drank part of it. She observed him while he drank it. When he stopped, she said, "Finish it all." So, he went back to drinking it until it was gone. "Good. Now come over here" and she walked over to another area just a few feet away. There was an odd-looking chair there. It was framed with square tube steel about an inch square and welded. It had arms that were padded, and the seat was two pads for the thighs, splayed into an extreme v shape, but there was nothing for the ass. There were also pads for the calf muscle and cups to put his heels into that were padded. There were also straps to secure every part of the body. 12 thought it looked like a steel version of an electric chair. She motioned for him to sit in it, and he did. He was surprised to find it quite comfortable and well designed for comfort even though his ass was not supported. Once he had adjusted himself to what he thought was the best position she began strapping him to the chair. He had not noticed it was on wheels, and she easily turned the chair to reach the straps on the other side rather than walking around the chair. She walked back over to the corner kitchenette and got another bottle of water and a pill bottle. Returning to 12 she opened the pill bottle and took out two little blue pills and two smaller yellow pills. Uncapping the bottle, she put the pills on his tongue and poured water in his mouth as he swallowed the pills. She went to the center of the room and grabbed a controller that hung from the overhead hoist that was tracked on the beam on the side of the room he was on. He could see that there was another hoist on the other side of the beam. That one was centered over a large table covered in black leather. She pulled the hoist along the beam and pressed a button on the controller. The motor hummed quietly as the cable came down to where she could reach the bright red hook on it. Letting go of the controller she went to a shelf and picked up some chains. 12 watched helpless and was more than a little afraid of what was going to happen. She attached chains to several points on the chair, then went back over to the shelves. Next to the wall she picked up a huge frame shaped in a six-foot x. it was 2-inch square tube, welded and there was a plate at the center of it which had an eye hook. The whole thing was chrome and it looked quite heavy. She lifted it up with no problem at all and hooked the hoist cable through the eye hook. Pulling the hoist over to 12, the frame was about three feet over his head. She attached the chains to the four corners of the frame where there were more eye hooks. She fussed with it a few moments until she had its level. Pushing the button on the controller she raised the chair, and 12, about six feet above the ground until his dangling cock which was getting hard was about at eye level to Gretchen. She let go of the controller and grabbed the chair and pulled it over to the center of the room. She went over to the door and grabbed the hose again and rolled it out to where she could hook the spray nozzle onto the center column. She grabbed a large oil drum with an open top on a four-wheel dolly and rolled it under 12's exposed ass. Grabbing the controller again she lowered the chair onto the drum. From the shelve she grabbed a box of blue latex surgical gloves and put a pair on her hands. Set down the box and grabbed a tube of jelly lube and a big red enema bottle that had a large aluminum nozzle. Lubed it very liberally before setting the lube back on the shelf and proceeded to insert the nozzle inside 12's ass. She hooked the enema bottle on the chain that held his chair. She reached up and grabbed his hairless balls gently with the lubed gloved hand, massaging his scrotum. She used her other hand to stroke his cock, which was very hard. He moaned from the pleasure of her attention. Then she stopped. She went back into the kitchenette and mixed a powder into a pitcher of warm water with wooden spoon. Then she returned and poured the solution into the enema bottle. Setting the picture down before she opened the clamp causing the flow into 12's bowels. Leaving it to gravity feed into him she then refilled the picture with warm water. She poured most of that into the bottle after a few minutes. The nozzle was large enough to seal the liquid inside of him, although some was leaking and dripping into the open top barrel. The pressure he felt in his bowels was uncomfortable, but his cock was straining. He felt embarrassed. Helpless. His mind was racing in confusion about what would happen. Why was Gretchen doing this? After a few minutes, she poured the rest of the water into the bottle. "Should not be very long now." She said looking 12 in his eyes. Just then the solution had begun to work, and he felt so full from it he was about to cry out. Suddenly the pressure pushed the nozzle out of his ass and all of his bowels voided into the barrel. The accompanying flatulence embarrassed 12 as did the disgusting odor. Gretchen grabbed the water hose and began to wash him off. She seemed unbothered as she directed the stream from the hose into his anus, washing any remaining debris away. He felt flushed and his head felt like his blood pressure was super high. He could feel his heart beating in his eyes.

When she was sure he was cleaned out, she used soap and a hand towel to gently wash his bottom side, his still hard cock, and his still sore balls. She used the hose to rinse him off good, then lifted the chair off of the barrel with the hoist. Moving the barrel over to a dump area she tipped it over and poured it into the drain. Using a sprayer, she washed the debris down the drain after rinsing out the barrel. She left it upside down on the steel bar grid over the drain.

Gretchen lowered his chair and unstrapped him. She helped him to stand up. The world started spinning and he fell into her arms. Out cold. Gretchen groaned with frustration.

Waking up in his bed was a surprise. 12 realized he must have passed out after the extreme cleansing that Gretchen gave him, if that were what you would call it. Gretchen must have carried him to his bed. That would not be a problem for her, he thought. She had in fact done exactly that. He wondered what time it was. He last remembered it was before dawn, but it was still dark outside. He had to pee, so he got up to use the restroom. As he stood in front of the commode and took a leak, the feel of his hairless body made him feel self-conscious. His skin felt oily all over, no doubt Gretchen had rubbed him down. He looked at the clock by his bed and saw that it was 5:20 am. He had not realized that he had been out for around twenty-four hours. He needed to brush his teeth and get over to the kitchen to meet Gretchen. He felt very hungry and very thirsty. After showering, 12 brushed his teeth and rinsed his mouth out. And headed out into the hallway. He could hear voices coming from the kitchen. When he got to the kitchen entrance, he saw that standing in the kitchen were two women that 12 didn't know and had never seen before. They were both nude, and they were both beautiful. One of them noticed him and smiled very big. She was thin and muscular, but had a small framed body and small breast with tiny nipples. Her hair was dark and long and flowed down her back in a ponytail. The other woman was about his height with ample breast with nipples that perked up so sharply you could hang your keys on them. Her hair was a strawberry blond color and fell down on her shoulders. She turned to see what the smaller breasted woman was smiling at, and she smiled big too after she saw him. "What do we 'Ave here?" she said in a British accent. She walked over to where he stood and put her right hand up to his head, grabbing his ear and pulling him into the room. "You just going to stand there ogling me when a man should be on his knees? ARE YOU?" and she pulled down on his ear until he went to his knees, then she let go. "I don't know who the hell you even are, but you sure as hell aren't going to stand at my level in front of me. Do you hear me? You're not."

The other woman stopped her and said "Hey, hey. Calm down. If the Queen has a man here, there must be a reason." She looked at her blond friend. She wasn't smiling now, and she had a look of worry in her eyes and glanced down at 12 who was so confused he didn't know what to do. "Why the 'ell would The Queen 'Ave a *man* here?" 12 thought the blond might not like men very much. He understood, really. He didn't much care for most of the men he had ever known either. "I am sure he is here because she wants him to be here, is all I am saying" she had New York accent. With that the blond softened her stance. "Oh. That hadn't occurred to me. Right you are. Okay you, back on your feet. Let's get a look at you." 12 began to stand up again. "There you go no harm done, right?" the British blond was smiling again "you took me by surprise. What's your name?" she stood back with her hands on her hips. "My name is 12." He said a little sheepishly. "Nice to meet you" she seemed confused for a moment only "nice to meet you too, 12. I am Mindy, and she is Cindy" the blond woman said. Cindy looked at him smiling her big smile and said "Hi!". Both Cindy and Mindy noticed that 12 had an erection beginning and them noticing wasn't making it any softer. Cindy reached out and patted his cock from the underside in her palm and said "He is so smooth. Look at this, he is getting a hard on." Cindy said smiling big. Mindy was just staring at 12's cock. She was getting aroused herself. She pinched her own right nipple in her right hand repeatedly. Cindy looked at Mindy and asked "Can I? He isn't collared or branded. Please?!" Sounding like a child asking for candy at the store. "Go ahead, Love." Mindy answered. With that Cindy fell to her knees and took 12's now hard cock into her mouth. 12 didn't know what to think. He wasn't prepared for this, and her mouth felt amazing as she deep throated him almost right away. He didn't last very long at all, cumming down her throat so hard he felt like he was going to fall down. She sucked his cock clean but didn't let go, she just kept sucking him, moving her head, grabbing his ass. Mindy was fingering herself and twisting her nipple like she was tuning in for a radio station. 12 moaned from the pleasure he was feeling. Cindy pulled him from her mouth and began bathing his balls with her tongue while she stroked him. To his amazement he was getting hard again. Cindy did not stop. Mindy came around behind 12 and pulled him by the shoulders down onto the floor until he was laying on his back. Cindy, now on her hands and knees, pulled his cock back into her mouth and slowly pumped him moving her head up and down. Mindy took position over 12 and lowered her neatly trimmed, dripping wet vagina onto his mouth. She put her hands on the floor above his head and her legs were spread quite wide. "Lick my pussy" she said as she moved it back and forth on his mouth. He was licking and sucking her juices from between her folds as Cindy was giving him a full-length stroke out of her mouth and back down again until the head of his cock was inside her throat. He could feel her moaning and the sound reverberated up his spine. He reached out with his hands and grabbed Mindy's ankles. She was shuddering on top of his face, and he heard her moaning as well. Mindy tensed up and began moving in a furious motion back and forth until she exploded in climax, her flow of juice filling his mouth and covering his face. He breathed it into his nose, it ran down into his ears. He felt it on his neck. He swallowed her cum. Then he also exploded, again, into Cindy's mouth. She pulled back until only the head of his shrinking cock was left in her mouth, and she sucked on it. Mindy got up from 12's face. She stood up. Cindy let 12's cock fall from between her lips, and it fell onto his stomach. She crawled up his body and gave him an open mouth kiss letting his ejaculate flow from her mouth into his. He tasted his own cum and swallowed it. That was a first, he thought. He was repulsed and turned on by it at the same time. It mixed with the taste of Mindy's nectar.   She licked the outside of his cheeks and mouth getting the flavor of Mindy on her tongue, before she rose to her knees and moved her own vagina over 12's mouth. She was wet and tasted very different than Mindy. But she also tasted nice. She rotated her hips back and forth while he licked her opening. She was pushing her clit against his nose. He darted his tongue in and out of her, it drove her crazy with pleasure. He couldn't smell anything but Mindy, however. He thought he was going to suffocate. He put his hands on her ass cheeks to help support her, but she just kept pushing down onto him. Cindy moaned quite loudly before she also came all over his face. When she was finished convulsing on him, she rose off of his face and smiled down at him. "Oh, it was so nice to meet you…. Hope it was good for you too." The two of them giggled as they left the kitchen, leaving 12 on the floor. Spent.

No sooner had Cindy and Mindy left, Gretchen walked into the kitchen catching 12 getting up from the floor. When he faced her, he saw her smirk a little, clearly curious as to what she had missed. She smelled the sex in the air, and she looked through the doorway and she could hear Cindy and Mindy giggling. "I see you met the girls." Gretchen said comically as she looked down at 12's shrunken manhood, clearly seeing the juice from them all over his face. Her face turned angry, and she said to him, in a low tone, "get your ass out of my kitchen and shower yourself! When you are finished get back in here and find me. I will make you pay for making me clean this mess off of my kitchen floor. You had better hurry. Don't make me come find you." His feet started to move but he slipped in the puddle of pussy juice Mindy had left around where 12's head had been, and if it wasn't for Gretchen reaching out and catching him under his left arm, he would have fallen. In one swift movement she lifted him up and brought her other hand on his ass five times. Each hit was harder than the last and he couldn't believe how hard she was hitting him with her bare hands. Tears welled up into his eyes and she said "GO!" as she let go of him. He ran to his room and brushed his teeth. He took a shower, soaping up head to toe, missing nothing, and rinsing off in what he was sure was record time. He dried himself off and rinsed his mouth with mouth wash. Then raced back to the kitchen to find Gretchen, Cindy, and Mindy all on their knees in front of an obviously angry Melissa. She looked at him. 12 froze in his tracks. When she continued to glare at him, he fell to his knees, a little harder than he should have, hurting his right knee in the process. "I am not happy, 12. You are not the one I hold responsible. You and I will have our own session later, right not I am correcting these GIRLS! Every one of you get on your feet right now and go to the stable. 12, you stay here with me for a moment. NOW!!" While 12 stayed on his knees, the others got up and walked quickly and quietly out the back door and headed to the stable. When they were gone, Melissa stood in front of 12, her legs apart. She was dressed in a white blouse and a white skirt. "Tell me what happened, 12. I want to understand it." 12 recounted every detail of what had happened in the kitchen this morning. Melissa tapped her foot in frustration. She was wearing white high heels that were not very high at all. "Look up at me 12, never advert your eyes from me or hang your head. I am going to tell you something, 12. I want you to remember it. I do not like it when someone uses my things without my permission. That goes for you as well." She wasn't yelling, but she was far from calm. She was serious. "Gretchen wasn't involved then?" she asked. "No, my Queen. She arrived after they left, like right after. I think she was pissed off too." 12 answered. She walked up to him and slapped him across the face with her right palm. "Don't get smart with me! You were not asked about what you think! Got that?" 12 was stunned but maintained his position "Yes my Queen" he said in a soft voice. "Stay right here, 12." And she turned and headed out the door in a huff. 12 did as he was told. He stayed on his knees even though it was very painful. He had actually managed to mess his right knee up. After about thirty minutes passed, Gretchen came back in the door. She still didn't look happy. "Get up, and put on your apron, 12. We will make breakfast." He was relieved. After tying his apron on, and washing his hands he asked her softly "What will happen?" Gretchen stopped and looked at him. He just could not tell what she was thinking. Her demeanor was totally unreadable. "What happens, happens, 12." She turned back to her task.

She was making omelets and toast. Together, they prepared the meal with no unnecessary conversation. When the meal was almost complete, Melissa came back inside the back door followed by Mindy and Cindy. They were all smiles, and it was just as if nothing had happened. "How much longer on breakfast, Gretchen?" Melissa asked, sounding chipper actually. 12 stood still, confused about what he was to be doing. "We are ready now, my Queen." Gretchen said "Marvelous, I am hungry" she looked at 12 "and I think we will all need our energy, so, let's all sit in the dining room and have breakfast." Melissa said as she headed for the dining room.

12 was so hungry he felt faint as he helped Gretchen bring out the plates already covered with omelets and toast. He thought to himself that this was the first time Melissa had taken breakfast in the dining room since he had been there. He normally served her in bed. Today was so not a normal day.

They all sat at the enormous table and began eating. Cindy and Mindy sat on one side of the table, Gretchen sat on the right of Melissa who sat at the head of the table. 12 sat on Gretchen's right side, across from Cindy.

"Cindy gives good blow jobs, don't you think so, 12?" Melissa said. She took a bite and looked at him. He blushed, panicked and felt very self-conscious all at the same time. Glancing at Cindy, he saw her smiling. She gave him a wink. He hung his head a little as he replied "yes, my Queen." Melissa never stopped looking at him. "Cindy and Mindy were both very impressed with your....... oral abilities. They told me so. I swear. I cannot keep her from blowing every cock she sees. This has happened before, and I expect it may happen again. But not with you, 12." She took another bite. 12 also took a bite. He didn't know what else to do, but he knew he was hungry. "She should have assumed that you were mine, 12. She knows now." Melissa continued "But not being marked at all, you were fair game I suppose. We will have to do something about that." Melissa took another bite then set her fork down and stood up from the table. "Finish your breakfast everyone. Cindy, Mindy… You girls have a lot of work to do. My pool has missed you, as have I. Gretchen. Prepare for a party, please. We will have guest over this evening. Say, around eight pm. Since everyone has already gotten to know 12, there is no need for further discussion this morning. 12, after you have finished your breakfast and cleaned the kitchen. Please join me…In the stable." And she turned and walked out of the room. Gretchen shot Cindy a look of contempt. Cindy smiled, but was clearly embarrassed. Mindy finished her breakfast first and rose from the table. "Come on you cock whore!" she said to Cindy grabbing her hair by the ponytail and pulling her up. Cindy was still smiling even though she clearly was in pain from her hair being pulled. "We have work to do!" and they left the room. Gretchen finished and getting up she turned and leaned down next to 12's face. "Wow." She said quietly, in a way that made 12 feel two inches tall. Then she walked away also.

12 put away the dishes after hand drying them. His knee was still hurting, but it had got a lot better. At least he hadn't broken it.

He could see through the kitchen window Mindy and Cindy working on the pool. They both had on bright yellow sleeveless jump suits that were tailor fit to their bodies. He thought that Mindy looked like a big slutty highlighter. Cindy's dark complexion made her look radiant in the yellow outfit. They were both beautiful women, he thought. In fact, 12 marveled at how he was surrounded by beautiful women. He truly felt lucky. Even though the punishment he would soon surely receive was on his mind, he felt lucky.

After he finished his task, he made a fast trip to freshen up then headed to the stable. He passed by the pool area and both Cindy and Mindy cooed and whistled at him. They were enjoying this, he thought. He stayed focused on getting to Melissa in the stable. The stable door was open. As he approached, he could see Melissa inside sitting on a stool, one foot on the floor, the other on the footrest of the stool. She was wearing a white leather corset that came over her breast. It had gold brads holding it and gold cord lace up the back snugging it to her perfect form. She wore white satin panties, a white garter belt holding up her white stockings. Her feet were clad in white satin ballet slippers. She looked stunning, he thought.

Melissa saw 12 approach and he rose from the stool. She saw that he was limping, favoring his right leg. He entered the stable and saw that they were alone. The room was well lit. He carefully lowered himself to his knees, taking care not to impact his sore knee. She walked up to him and ran her fingers thru his hair. She pulled his head against her stomach and hugged his head. They stayed like that for a few minutes, the closeness they felt for one another obvious to them both. "What happened to your leg, 12?" she asked genuinely concerned. "I fell onto it too hard kneeling back at the kitchen, my Queen." She ran her nails up his neck, then gently grabbed his left ear. The sensations of being stroked and the fact that he was still getting used to having zero body hair were causing arousal. She broke away from the embrace and went over and closed the door. Taking him by the hand she led him over to the very large, low table. "Here, sit down." He sat down on the padded leather. Melissa ran her palms over his hairless chest and down his stomach. "So smooth. I like it." He thought that her hands felt amazing. Whenever she touched him, her touch felt like love to him. She was standing in front of him and leaned down and kissed his lips, biting his lower lip firmly but gently. In her left hand she rubbed his injured knee, but her right hand found his cock. She kissed him again, and he returned her kiss. She held his erection, but didn't stroke it. She didn't squeeze it, she just held it while her kisses became more passionate. She was rubbing his knee, and her hand felt amazing. "How do you like being here? Would you like to stay with me or move on to someplace else? *Someone* else? You are not a prisoner, 12. I want you to be happy and satisfied" she asked him, still holding his cock in her hand. "I love it here with you, my Queen. I want to stay with you." He felt like he may not have understood the question. It was after all the first time she had asked him what he thought or wanted since he had been there. The days were full of him attending her needs, being trained and corrected harshly or being tasked by Gretchen. She seemed to like whipping him, at least a little, every day. The way he felt while she whipped him was loved. Her whip caused pain, pleasure and emotions that sometimes overwhelmed him. He was accustomed to being nude all the time, he felt good about himself. She made him feel good about himself. "May I ask a question my Queen?" he so badly wanted her to move her hand on his cock, but she just held it. "Didn't you just do that anyway?" she kissed him again a little laugh while her tongue was still in his mouth. She had a quick wit, and he loved her laugh. "Yes, 12. You can ask me a question." She moved her hand off of his knee and held the side of his face. Her other hand squeezed his cock a little. She was looking into his eyes. "Have you been happy with me?" he asked. He really wanted to know. To hear her say it. He wanted her to be happy with him and he would do anything, anything at all if she told him to. She didn't respond. Her grip on his cock increased slightly as she pinched his nipple. She lowered her head and sucked on his other nipple, biting it. Gently at first, then harder. His erection was very stiff in her hand and now he was desperate for her to stroke him. She moved her mouth away, blew on his nipple, then licked it back and forth. He lifted his hand from the table to touch her, but she rose up grabbing his wrist and pushed his hand back down with force. "Watch it, hands!" she said softly but sternly. She kissed him again, then let go of his cock. She walked away from him towards a roll around cart that had some bdsm gear on it, and selected a pair of leather fur lined wrist cuffs. They were the type that had buckles and a ring to attach a lock. Exactly the same kind Gretchen had put him in. She came over and put them on him one at a time. When she had finished, she went back to the cart and returned with some chains that had a clasp to attach to the cuffs he was now wearing. "Lay down on your back." She ordered. 12 did as he was told, his erection pointing straight up. She attached the chain and pulled his left arm over to the corner of the large table and attached it to a ring mounted to the table leg. She repeated the same for his right arm. He was now chained to the table laying on his back. Then she did the same thing to both of his legs. She made the chains tight, and he couldn't move at all. The table was so large that even with his legs spread and his arms spread out above his head there was about twenty inches of chain on the table attached to each corner. There was no hope of reaching any of the clasps. "Now I would tell you to just relax, but I really don't want you to." She reached out and grabbed his testicles quite firmly with her left hand. He winced as she squeezed them. She pulled them using both hands. She picked up a small flogger, a miniature version of the flogger she used on him sometimes and he watched helplessly as she beat him on the balls with it. He tried not to, but the pain was so intense he yelped on almost every stroke. She alternated between hitting the underside of his inexplicably hard cock, and his balls. He would have never thought in his life that such a small little whip could cause that much pain. He hated that whip the most. This was the worst Melissa had ever hurt him. She was always accurate in causing pain, she had never damaged him. He trusted her completely, but she surely must be going too far this time. He was crying now, but she didn't stop. "Oh please! Oh, please no! please stop!" he pulled to get away, but it was useless. She must have hit his cock and balls fifty or maybe even a hundred times. He couldn't see but he felt like he might be bleeding. Melissa was smiling when she finally stopped. His balls and cock were on fire, but he had managed not to use his safe word. He was closer than he had ever been though. His balls had turned beet red from the abuse, but they were not bleeding. "There. Now how do you feel? Feel like sticking that cock in anyone's mouth? I bet..... you...... do....... not." She hit him again on each syllable she said. She climbed on top of him, they were face to face. "I want you to remember this, 12. You might think that cock and those balls are yours, but they are not. They are mine. You aren't to use them without my permission. You use them when I want you to use them. And another thing I want you to know, if I have too, I will have them removed. Cut off. I am quite serious, 12. As much I like MY cock, I will cut it off. I would rather not, however, so let's try to keep MY COCK and MY BALLS from becoming a problem! Okay?" she waited perhaps a minute and he hadn't responded. He was in such pain he didn't actually realize that she wanted a response, or even that she had asked him a question. He was thinking about that crazy woman who cut off her husband's dick and threw it out the car window. The thought scared him. The pain was intense. The tears in his eyes blurred his vision, and the pain he felt in his balls made his head full of pressure. "Okay?" she asked again patiently. "Yes, my Queen!" he answered quickly and urgently. She down laid at his side and put her hand on his aching balls and gently caressed them. He winced at first. She put her cheek on his still heaving chest. She could hear his heart pounding. She moved her hand to his still hard cock, gripped it lightly and pumped it up and down. Then the pain suddenly and completely stopped. He felt a rush of pleasure as she stroked him slowly, watching her hand on his, or rather her, cock pumping it up and down. She had not planned to, but she suddenly wanted it in her mouth. She rose up on the table and turned to face the bright red and purple cock and put her lips on the head. She licked all around the head before lowering her mouth on him taking the full length. He couldn't believe what he was feeling, how the pain was now replaced by ecstasy. He was sure he would not last long before cumming. But then, as he couldn't comprehend what was happening, she suddenly stopped. His cock was now throbbing, standing straight up and swollen to the limit. She rose to her knees still straddling him and lowered her soaked, satin panty clad pussy on to his face, then rocked back and forth. Rubbing her clit from his chin to his nose, then back again. He loved the feel of her satin panties with her moist pussy coming thru against his face. Her heady aroma filled his nostrils and the flavor of her on his lips was sweet. He loved the way she tasted. She moaned only slightly as she tensed up and exploded in orgasm, speeding up her motion, and putting more pressure on his face. She stopped suddenly and lifted herself off of him, then climbed down off of the table. 12's face was drenched in her essence.

Melissa stood next to the table. She took her panties off and climbed back on top of him. She expertly guided his cock inside her wet pussy and lowered herself down onto him, facing away from him, reverse cowgirl. He had a wonderful view of her ass. She leaned forward onto her elbows which pulled his cock with her downward towards his feet. She began thrusting herself back and forth, bending her shoulders leaving her forearms and hands flat on the leather covered table between his cuffed, spread and chained legs. The downward angle his cock was pointing put pressure on him that was not pleasant, and when she bottomed out on his shaft, his testicles pressed on her clit. She did it harder and harder causing him pain. Her pussy felt amazing. As she orgasmed, she squeezed him so hard he thought he might pass out. She rode him harder and faster until she came again, this time causing his explosive climax. He screamed out in pain and pleasure. He filled her pussy with spasm after spasm of his cum, and she bore down on him pushing him as far inside of her as she could and climaxed again, 12's screams pushing her ecstasy over the edge. Feeling him ejaculate hot spurts inside her causing her to scream of pleasure and thrust with furious motion. Suddenly, she stopped with his cock buried deep inside her. They stayed that way for several minutes, spent. She rose up off of him and his still half hard cock. She turned and repositioned her pussy over 12's mouth and lowered herself down. "Clean me with your tongue, now" she commanded softly. He started licking. She bore her pussy down harder. He felt his cum filling his mouth. For the second time in his life, and the second time that day, he swallowed his own cum. The taste of her pussy combined with the taste of his cum was interesting. Being forced to swallow his cum disgusted him in a way, but also turned him on to do it for her. "Suck it out, slave." She said in a low growling tone. This really turned him on. He felt humiliated, and he also felt more submissive than he had ever felt before. He loved the feeling of being told how and what to do. Being controlled. Suffering dutifully for her. He loved her for fulfilling his dreams of being a slave for a powerful woman. But the thought of her cutting off his dick bothered him. He always took her seriously. Would she actually do something like that? This was more than he bargained for.

The term "slave" had bothered him once upon a time, even though he always desired to be one. He learned in academy that his being a "consensual slave" was not the same thing as what the word historically meant. The term was simply an aid for his headspace, and for simplicity. He did know that he could say his safe word at any time and that everything would stop until the problem was resolved and a new understanding reached.

Melissa moved her sex on his face lightly before lifting away. He looked up at her and saw that she was smiling. "I waited a long time for that, 12." She said looking down at him. "Thank you, my Queen." 12 responded.

After Melissa put ice packs on 12's cock and balls, she picked up her panties and walked out of the stable, leaving him chained to the table. He was in terrible pain. He started to cry. The ice packs caused a new discomfort, and he soon began to shiver. As if the ice was freezing his blood. After what felt like an hour he finally relaxed enough to doze off. He heard music playing in the distance, and the commotion of people talking and laughing. He thought it was a dream until Gretchen released the chain from the fur lined cuffs on his wrist. She then removed the now melted ice packs. She walked over and put the baggies of water in the sink, then returned to 12 and released his ankle chains too. "Stay right here, 12." Gretchen said. She went over to the sink again and ran some water into a large stainless-steel bowl. She took a few towels off a shelf and returned to 12. She began washing his cock and balls with great care. The pain had subsided, but his balls were still tender. There was a dull ache. 12 could hear a man outside talking and laughing quite loudly. "Who is that?" 12 asked Gretchen who seemed to ignore his question, but after a minute she answered "Guest of our Queen, 12. You are to be very respectful of all of her guest. I want you to remember. You are not to say anything, do not utter a word to anyone, unless Queen Melissa tells you to speak. And if she does, you need to use as few words as you can. No one other than Queen Melissa, understand me?" Gretchen had him sit up but maintained her eye contact with him. "Yes, Gretchen. I understand." She continued washing him "you must not embarrass your Queen, her guest may have their way with you. Obey their demands, whatever it may be. You are not to resist any of them. Some of them have brought their own servants as well. You will be able to spot them as they will be nude. It is the rules. Servants are to remain nude. You may not make any contact with any other servants, unless instructed to do so by a guest. But even then, remember not to udder a word to anyone other than your Queen." Gretchen started drying him off. His knee didn't hurt him until he tried to stand. He winced from the pain. Gretchen nodded but didn't say a word. She went to the fridge, got out two bottles of water and a pill bottle and returned. She handed him the water and took out two blue and two yellow pills, it looked to 12 like the same pills she gave him before. He took the pills, drank the water without a word. "Good" Gretchen said, not looking at him beyond him swallowing. She picked up a jar and removed the lid. There was a cream inside. She started at his neck and began rubbing the cream all over his body. She stood him up so she could get his ass. It was bright white with gold sparkles inside of it. She rubbed it over every square inch of him but his face and his genitals. His cock and balls stopped aching. He looked weird, hairless white sparkled body. She looked at the clock, making note of the time.

They emerged from the stable at exactly 9 o'clock he walked in front of Gretchen. His wrist and ankles wearing the cuffs, but not chained or leashed. They walked towards the pool area and the small crowd of about 10 people. Some were in fact nude. The ones who were clothed, a mix of men and women, wore mask. They were all formally dressed. The men had tuxedos and the ladies wore beautiful gowns. There was soft music coming from speaker disguised as rocks in the landscaping. He recognized the song playing as a Clapton hit, "Layla" Clapton sang.

The entire crowd stopped their conversations and watched 12 and Gretchen approach. 12 noticed that while all the men wore a smooth, white face mask, the women wore different decorative feather masks that covered the upper part of their faces only. 12 did not know who any of these people might be, so he assumed that the masks were for their own benefit, not his. He spotted Queen Melissa. She was not wearing any sort of mask either. She had on a very beautiful white gown. She smiled large when she saw him approach. When he got to her, she made a hand gesture for Gretchen, who was behind him, and Gretchen disappeared inside the house. Melissa looked at 12 up and down and smiled. "Kneel, 12." She said in a very happy tone. As he knelt down beside her, she put her right hand on top of his head and turned back to a guest she was talking to. "He was a gift to me by dear friends who unfortunately could not be here tonight. I have decided to make him a permanent addition with me. I am rather fond of him, and he takes to my training well." Melissa was playing with his hair as she spoke. "He isn't too old? He isn't exactly in prime condition either." the woman in front of Melissa asked. She was wearing a pink gown and her mask was made from pink feathers. Her skin was pale and her hair red, 12 didn't like her and he thought she looked like a Florida trailer park bimbo, although he would never say that even if asked what he thought, which was an unlikely event anyway. "Well, I thought he might be at first, I have changed my mind about that. You should too, Sil." Melissa never broke her smile, but she did turn toward the overweight man that was with her and offered to him "You look marvelous in that tux, Charles. How is your business doing? Still taking advantage of unsuspecting people looking to save for retirement?". The man's mouth dropped open in shock, Melissa didn't wait for a response from the portly man before continuing "I thank you for coming tonight, but I think it would be best if you left. Now." Melissa said smiling politely as she raised her hand and suddenly Gretchen appeared out of nowhere "Gretchen will show you to your car. Charles. Silvia. Good evening." Melissa didn't move from where she stood as Gretchen extended her hand, motioning for them to follow her, which they both did without so much as a word. The small gathering of people was completely silent as the couple disappeared around the corner of the house with Gretchen walking behind them making certain that they didn't get lost. 12 blushed. "Stand up, 12." Melissa said. And he did as she instructed. Melissa looked him in the eye and as she smiled, she winked at him "No loss." She whispered to 12 and she reached over and grabbed his cock. She turned and began walking up to the deck, leading him by his cock behind her.

From the elevated position of the deck 12 could make out there were three slaves, one male and two female. They were with different guest. The female slaves were kneeling next to their owners and the male slave was on his hands and knees facing the ground. He was wearing some type of harness around his head that had a leash attached to it, and he appeared to have a tail coming out of his ass that curled straight up. Just then 12 wondered where Mindy and Cindy were. "Kneel, 12." He did as Melissa asked. He heard the back door open and as 12 was now facing this crowd of masked strangers, he was unable to see Mindy and Cindy come out of the house taking up position on the other side of Melissa.

"Thank you all for coming tonight" Melissa said very clearly and loud, but not shouting. "It is my wish that you all enjoy yourself. The first thing on our program today is my offering to you, two female slaves for open bid." Melissa turned and 12 could see Mindy and Cindy standing to the left of Melissa. They were also in white body color with gold glitter just as 12 was, with their faces and genitals left uncovered. They both had their breast covered in the cream. Mindy was holding a box in both hands. Neither girl was smiling.

"But that is for later, get to know them. They come as a pair, no bidding on them separately. There will be an auction for them two hours from now." Melissa walked over behind the two girls but continued "What you see is what you get. Two beautiful girls who both are very bisexual and eager to please. I start the bidding at two hundred." Melissa took the box from Mindy and continued "Go mingle, girls" and Mindy and Cindy obediently walked down the steps together into the pool area to the crowd of masked people.

Melissa returned to 12 and continued. "The second thing on our program is this male right here. 12." She looked at him smiling. His heart sank. Was she going to sell him? He panicked. He could hear his heart beating. "I am going to collar him. If he will take my collar." He was looking at her as she opened the box and produced a thin gold round bar collar. "Will you take my collar 12?" she asked him. He tried to answer but his words wouldn't come out. Finally, he was able to answer, emotionally, "Yes, my Queen. I will wear your collar. Proudly." There was an outburst of applause and laughter. They all seemed happy about this, but not as happy as 12. Melissa opened the very smooth gold collar that had a very hidden hinge and locking latch and put it around 12's neck. She closed it and used a small tool to tighten something at the latch. It felt cool against his skin, and had weight to it despite it being thin. It fit perfect, not loose and dangling and not tight either. Melissa smacked his ass with her hand and said loudly for everyone to hear "You are mine, 12." Again, there were applause. 12 felt tears in his eyes. He didn't know what to do, he just looked up at her and smiled at her. She raised her hand and again the crowd fell quiet. "We will return, but for now please, enjoy the party." Melissa put out her hand and 12 rose to his feet. She grabbed him by his cock and led him into the house. After he closed the door behind him, she led him into her bedroom, and closed the door. She kissed him, holding his head in both of her hands. He returned her kiss, passionately. She began removing her gown and he helped her. When she was naked, she sat on the bed and he went down to his knees in front of her when she pointed at her pussy, leaning back on her elbows. He leaned in and licked her from the bottom of her sex to the top, his tongue wide and pushing open her folds. She was wet with excitement. He savored the way she tasted on his lips as he flicked his tongue on her clit. She moaned loudly and jerked with each flick of his exquisite tongue as electricity shot thru her. His hands found her breast and he squeezed them as he sucked her clit into his mouth. She grabbed his hair and pulled his face against her pussy and began directing his head into her and up and down, bucking her hips in the opposite motion. She stopped suddenly and orgasmed screaming out loudly. "Fuck me 12, now!" he stood up and his cock was rock hard. He entered her slowly, feeling her velvety wet pussy. He held her legs up as she laid on her back, her hair around her head. He thrust into her repeatedly, each time he hit her clit she came closer and closer to another orgasm. She came again and he didn't stop. She screamed in pleasure, her eyes wide as he pounded her furiously until he couldn't hold back anymore, and he shot his cum inside of her. They both collapsed, spent. 12 wondered to himself how life could be better than this. Melissa thought that she had never gotten a gift as wonderful as 12, and she smiled as she fell asleep planning her day with 12 tomorrow, and what she was going to do to him.

Cup the Balls

They laid there for some time, bodies wrapped in each other on the crisp white cotton sheets of Queen Melissa's king size bed. 12's head was on her stomach, and he was in that dreamy after sex euphoria that was as surely as close to God as anyone could be here on Earth. She had both hands holding and caressing his head. She too, was feeling blissful. His new collar around his neck was laying against her and the fact that he was wearing it made her warm inside. She had not collard a man since her late husband. She tried not to think of him, but it was impossible. Only because she had not been this happy since then. She had made peace with his loss, and even found herself to be a happy person, but this was something more. 12 was something more. The way he made her feel. His dutiful commitment to her was intoxicating. Some slaves simply endure, they serve. Some are not even very good at that, she thought. She smiles to herself at how her life has changed since being gifted 12.

When the knock at the bedroom door startled both of them, Melissa groaned out loud then said, "What is it, Gretchen?" knowing it was her. Even knowing what she wanted before she said it. "Your guest are waiting, my Queen. Do you have any instructions for me?" Gretchen said from outside the door. Melissa thought about that for a minute. "Yes Gretchen. Would you please inform them that I shall be with them momentarily? Then please see to 12 for me. I want him bathed clean and his cock locked, then bring him to me wherever I am, please Gretchen." Melissa said kindly as she untangled herself from both 12 and the bedsheets. "Of course, my Queen." Gretchen replied. 12 rose out of the bed and as he stood, she stood with him, pulled his face to hers and gave him a long, deep kiss. They embraced each other. Her breast against him caused his cock to stiffen again. Feeling that she reached down and grabbed his cock and said "I am going to make sure this stays safe. Go with Gretchen now." She let go of him and slapped his ass. "Yes, my Queen." 12 said as he turned and walked out of the room to find Gretchen waiting for him. She took him to her room to carry out Melissa's orders.

When Melissa was dressed, she rejoined the party. She took in what was going on, her hands on her hips. She wasn't particularly surprised to see Cindy on her knees in front of a couple of men who had their cocks out for her. She knew how much of a cock whore that girl was. But seeing Mindy on her back being fucked by a man while licking a woman's pussy did surprise her. The man pulled his enormous prick out of her and sprayed her and the woman straddling her face with an extra ordinarily large amount of his cum. This apparently caused the woman over Mindy to climax and shudder with ecstasy. She screamed in pleasure before stopping her movements and rising from Mindy's face. The man rose from between her legs. And Mindy just laid there. She was obviously spent. Cindy was working hard on sucking one big cock while she was stroking the other man who wasn't as well endowed. The man being stroked climaxed and came on Cindy's breast, but Cindy never stopped sucking the other man. She simply let go of the now shrunken little penis and used that hand to cup the balls of the man she was enjoying. The man who was fucking Mindy brought his female slave over and told her to lick Mindy clean of his semen that he left on her breast and neck, and stomach. She seemed to really like it because she licked Mindy enthusiastically until she was clean. Mindy made a face then giggled.

The guest who had the male slave with the dog tail butt plug were playing fetch with him. They were holding drinks and talking as they tossed a stick for him to chase after. When he returned on all fours with the stick he held in his mouth, shaking his ass causing the rubber tail to wag like a dog's tail would. They would take their time and pat his head before taking the stick from his mouth and then tossing it again, the dog boy scrambling after it on his hands and knees.

There were a few women just sitting at a table having drinks. They laughed and chatted amongst themselves. When they spotted Melissa, they waved her over to them. Melissa walked over to where they were near the pool. "Are you enjoying yourselves ladies?" Melissa asked them "We sure are, and thank you for having us, Queen Melissa." The older blond woman said. The younger red head spoke up "and congratulations on your new collard male! We were just talking about how we haven't known you to have many male slaves, and you haven't collard any, are we right?" Melissa looked at her. The question angered her, but she could see that it was actually an innocent question. Not a judgmental one. Still, she bit her tongue, held her breath a moment before responding. "Thankyou. But to answer your question, no. I had one long ago. My husband. He has passed. I really don't care to talk about that, however. You'll understand." Melissa maintained a stoic face. The women picking up on her body language quickly agreed and apologized. "Well 12 looks to be quite the find. I am happy for you!" the red head said again "Mike and I came for your auction actually hoping to find a male such as 12, for me. He is the one down there with the girl you are auctioning. He is trying her out. I told him we cannot take on two females right now, though they both seem to be very quality slaves." Melissa looked over to see Cindy still working that large cock into her mouth. Melissa smiled "Her name is Cindy." Melissa said "And, it seems as if she has met her match. She loves giving head. I swear I can't keep her from trying to suck every male that she comes in contact with. Is he ever going to cum?" They all laughed, and the red head said "He is a freak of nature. He can just keep going and going until I tell him he can cum." She stood up and shouted "Mike! Cum already!" then she sat back down. Melissa watched as he grabbed Cindy's head in both hands and threw his head back as he pumped deep into her throat, and he yelled as he spasmed and ejaculated right down her throat. Cindy's eyes were wide, and she held him by his ass cheeks as he pulled his still half hard and still quite large cock out of her mouth. Melissa noticed Mike's cock had a huge bright red head, and Cindy licked it and kissed it and stroked it to get any remaining semen out of it. "My goodness his cock is huge. I am sure he keeps you happy, Mary." The red head laughed again, but the other two women just stared at Mikes cock with their mouths slightly hanging open. Mary and Melissa both noticed this and shared a laugh together. "Please excuse me, ladies." Melissa said and turned to walk away as they all said "Of course, Queen Melissa."

Melissa clapped her hands and said loudly for everyone to hear "Okay everyone if I can get your attention, please." The noise died down as everyone turned towards her. Cindy and Mindy both hurried to Melissa's side, and with a motion of Melissa's hands they knelt on each side of her facing the guest. The white and gold coloring rubbed off on almost all of both their bodies. They had certainly been inspected, Melissa thought to herself. The door opened and 12 came out onto the deck, and instinctually took up a spot kneeling next to Mindy on Melissa's right side. "I will get right to it. First, thank you all for being here, I am glad you shared this special event with me. Doesn't 12's collar fit him nicely?" Melissa turned and pointed to 12. "Notice, also his Chastity cage he will wear for me. That is at this time for his benefit." The small crowd applauded and cheered. "Secondly, I am going to exercise my prerogative to change my mind, and cancel the auction of these two girl slaves, who have served me wonderfully. I have had a change of heart and simply do not wish to part with them." Both Cindy and Mindy exhaled and smiled. They literally beamed with delight. There was reluctant applause but no cheers at that. "I know, I know. Some of you had your heart set on them. Perhaps in the future you may have this opportunity again, but for now at least, I am keeping them with me for further training." There was more applause at that. "As I said, I appreciate you coming tonight. With that, I am brining this evening to a close. Please do not feel the need to linger. We will see you all very soon at the next event! Thank you, and good night." Melissa turned and waved over to the red headed woman "Mary, could I have a word with you, please?" and Mary nodded yes and walked over to Melissa. They talked for a moment and Mary began to laugh, grabbing her stomach and saying "Yes! of course!" loudly to Melissa. She motioned her husband to come over. Melissa turned and said "12, go fetch Gretchen for me, have her meet me in the stable, then help the girls clean up this mess. Girls, I will talk to you in the morning. 12, After this mess is all clean come meet me in the stable. The girls are going to shower and go to bed." Melissa said pointing at all of the debris from the party. "Are we all clear as to what I want?" Melissa asked and the three of them answered together almost musically "Yes my queen." The girls giggled at how it sounded together, but 12 was already headed in the door to find Gretchen.

Melissa told Mary and Mike "Please come with me." Pointing down the path to the stable. Mary took Mike by his arm and told him

"Come on with us. This will be fun!" and he smiled and walked with them to the Stable. When Melissa opened the door and turned on the lights his eyes grew wide with what he saw inside. "Mary what is this? What is going on here? What do you two have planned?" Mike said with increasing alarm as he looked at the fully appointed dungeon. Some of what he saw made him excited, but some of the items distressed him. He wasn't a submissive bottom. He was a dominate top and he had no plans of being whipped. "Mike, just remember what we have agreed. I let you play with that girl slave in front of everyone tonight. That's exactly what has led you here. Now you have had yours, I am going to have mine. Agree with me right now, or we will have to redefine the nature of our marriage." Mary looked at him quite sternly as she continued "Because you pulled out your big dick and showed off to everyone, everyone took notice, and now Queen Melissa wants your big dick. On her terms. You are going to do everything she says, and I am going to be here to make sure you do. Understand me?!" Mike thought about all of that for only a couple of seconds before saying "Oh! Well Okay then! I am game." Looking at Queen Melissa who was smiling at him. Gretchen opened the door and walked in closing the door behind her. "Come over here and take off all your clothes please, then set them on the bench here." Melissa told him. Gretchen turned around and locked the door on the inside. That made Mike even more nervous, but he did what was asked of him. Gretchen picked up a pair of the fur lined wrist cuffs and walked over to Mike who was half finished undressing. He was keeping a wary eye on Gretchen. Mary sat down in a chair facing them and said "Oh don't get all shy now, Mike. Hurry up and get naked!" Mike shot her a look but continued to undress, taking off his underwear and socks. Gretchen reached out and took his left hand and buckled the leather cuff on it, then she took his right hand and repeated the task. She reached over her head and pulled a chain attached to the hoist until it was low enough to attach his cuffs to the clasp. He was then powerless to move. Gretchen then went to a cabinet in the kitchenette and produced a pill bottle and a glass. Filled the glass with water, while whistling pleasantly. She returned over to where Mike stood with his arms suspended, loosely, above his head with both of his wrist attached to a single hook. "Stick out your tongue." Gretchen told him softly. He reluctantly did and Gretchen placed a blue pill on his tongue and then held up the glass of water to his lips. "Swallow." Gretchen said softly, slowly pronouncing each syllable individually. Mike could see she wasn't going to discuss it with him, so he did as he was told. "GOOD! Good boy!" Gretchen told him as she poured the remaining water on his head. He shook his head and said "Hey! What the hell? What's your problem?" But Gretchen just ignored him. Melissa and Mary laughed at that. "Gretchen, I think we should do his ankles too." Melissa said while she laughed at his reddening face. "Yes, my Queen." Gretchen answered, and went to get a cart from another part of the room. She returned with the cart and reached up to grab the controls, hit the button with the up arrow on it and raised the cable and hook until his feet were off the floor and his stomach was at eye level to Gretchen. Gretchen attached fur lined cuffs to his ankles, then attached a spreader bar to both cuffs. Mike was wiggling and cursing her under his breath at this point. Gretchen was undeterred and didn't even acknowledge his resistance. Mary and Melissa watched as this was going on when Mary said "This is an impressive dungeon you have. I love it." Melissa turned away from Mike's predicament and simply said, "Thanks."

12 tried to enter the locked door to the stable, and upon realizing it was locked he knocked three times lightly. Melissa walked over and let him in. After he was inside, she locked the door again. 12 looked at Mike and his situation. Mike didn't look very happy as Gretchen lowered the hoist until his feet touched the green tiled floor, enough that he could put some weight on them, but not enough to be flat on the floor. She began getting some materials together from the kitchenette as he dangled there, helpless to move. She returned and began shaving his pubic hair completely off.

Melissa walked back over to where Mary was sitting in a chair and motioned for 12 to follow her over there. "12, kneel here facing Mistress Mary." Melissa pointed to a spot about three feet in front of Mary, and 12 knelt on it. He looked at Mary who was also eyeing him and his chastity device. She leaned forward to get a better look at it but didn't say anything. Mike was watching to see what was happening. Melissa walked over to Mike and looked at his penis, which was soft, but still large. She reached down and lightly grabbed it, giving it a couple strokes. She cupped his balls with her left hand and gently squeezed them. She made no eye contact with Mike at all and turned around and returned over to where 12 was looking at Mary. "Mary, would you like for 12 to lick you orgasm? He is quite skilled." Melissa asked the red-haired woman, smiling. "Oh, that would be wonderful! Thank you!" She rose up and started to undress. "Here you can hang your clothes over here pointing to a rack with hooks. Melissa also undressed, and the two women both hung their clothes on the hooks. They looked at each other's bodies and began to caress each other. They ran their hands over each other's breast before embracing in a kiss. They didn't kiss long, and Melissa led Mary by the hand over to the large table, and motioned for 12 to follow her. Mary sat down on the edge, but Melissa stood over her as 12, crawling on his hands and his knees, arrived between Mary's knees as she spread them for him. Melissa watched as Mary put her hands on 12's head and pulled him down to her moist pussy and he began lightly licking her. She laid back on the table and Melissa sat on the edge next to Mary. She watched 12 as he softly ran his flat tongue over Mary's sex. Melissa leaned over and kissed Mary's firm nipples. She sucked each of them in alternately and played with them with her tongue. Mary moaned in pleasure. Gretchen was mixing something in a large mixing bowl and watching the action.

Gretchen poured the solution she was mixing into a large, long metal cylinder that had a metal rectangular base at the top. It had eye hooks at all four corners of the base. She set it on a custom-made stand on the cart so the solution wouldn't spill. She walked over to Mike and lowered the hoist. She then attached another chain to his wrist cuffs. She pulled the cart over and tested the consistency of the solution she had poured into the cylinder by sticking her finger into it. Shaking her head slightly she went and wheeled over a bench that had a padded top for him to lay onto and on each side, it had a padded ledged for him to put his legs. "Lay down here." She said pointing at the top pad as she pulled the chain attached to his wrist. Mike was so glad not to be suspended any longer he gladly did what he was told, watching Mary in ecstasy as 12 and Melissa both pleasured her. His cock was rock hard, and he longed to stroke it. Gretchen attached his wrist cuffs to each side of the spanking bench. She then grabbed his penis and stroked it. She then pushed his large hard cock into the cylinder. The rectangle portion filled with the solution and covered his testicles. Gretchen then attached straps around Mike and to the eye hooks on the penis mold his cock was currently inside so that it would stay put. He then felt her remove the spreader bar and attached his legs securely to the sides of the spanking bench. Mike felt like his cock and balls were on fire and started to moan and the feeling just kept getting worse. He thought she has put his cock in acid or something. And he tried to get up with no success. "Be still!" Gretchen told him. "It is just the muscle cream I mixed into the mold solution. It helps you stay your hardest while the mold works on your penis. It is my own recipe, and it works well don't you think? Of course, the pill I gave you will help too." And with that she slapped his ass hard. Mike yelped in pain, but he never took his eyes off Mary who was now kissing Melissa while 12 licked her to ecstasy.

Mary shuddered as she climaxed again and again, pulling 12's head and thrusting against his mouth and face. Then she quickly pushed his head away from her sensitive vagina. He pulled back and moved towards Melissa to give her pussy a thorough licking when Mary pulled Melissa up to her and dove between her legs and started licking her. Melissa moaned in pleasure. Her left foot was in front of 12 and he started licking and sucking her toes while supporting her leg in his hands. Mary was on her elbows supporting Melissa's ass cheeks in her hands as she sucked Melissa's pussy into her mouth, licking deep into her folds. Melissa ran her hands thru Mary's hair.

When Melissa orgasmed, she exploded in screams of pleasure, her body shaking. Mary withdrew and laid down beside her. Melissa had pulled her leg away from 12 and he knelt beside the leather clad table. He was very happy. What a wonderful day, he thought to himself. Mike's whimpers of pain and discomfort eventually got Mary's attention, and she got up and went over there to him. "Are you okay, Honey?" Mary asked him. "It burns!" Mike answered her. He sobbed and exhaled after saying that. Gretchen was standing behind him, keeping a close eye on the mold and making sure he didn't move. "How much longer?" Mary asked her. "Five more minutes." Gretchen answered. "Then I will be done with him." Melissa was getting dressed. "Come along 12, we are going to bed, Mary talks to you later, okay? I will call you. Mike. Thank you for your contribution to my collection. Gretchen, tomorrow 12 and I are sleeping in. Please don't wake us." Melissa said. 12 rose to his feet and followed his Queen. She unlocked the door and then looking back out the door she said, "Goodnight, everyone" Gretchen and Mary both said, "Goodnight my Queen." Mike just moaned in pain, and everyone laughed.

Making their way up the path from the stable Melissa and 12 walked quietly. 12 followed her closely, reaching up to feel his collar. He had never been so happy as he was. The scent of Mary still in his nostrils. He preferred the scent of his Queen. Reaching the house, she told him "I am so proud of you, 12. You will sleep with me for now on. I am exhausted! So, lets hurry up and shower and get into bed." He was tired too, and a little relieved when she said that. He simply said, "As you wish, my Queen." It had been exactly two years since he began on this journey. Now he knew he made the right choice. His fears not realized. While they showered together and got into bed, almost wordless, he remembered how this all began.

Twelve

I sat in my Honda, with twenty-five thousand dollars in a manila envelope in my hands. I knew the chances of getting what I wanted were likely pretty slim. I was most likely making the biggest mistake of my life. And was about to pay an embarrassing price for my stupidity. But whatever. I wasn't happy. I was alone. If I was murdered and buried in the desert, nobody would really miss me. I felt like I had more to offer. Like I could be of use to someone besides myself.

Mistress Raven sounded genuine enough, but perhaps I had just read too much erotic fiction. I owed myself the chance, though. So, I went through with it. I was to meet a driver at the Reno airport. I had put everything I owned in storage, paid for two years up front. I was instructed to bring the cash, told to put it in a specific envelope. I was told where to park, even which space number to park in. Parking space number 12.

Twenty minutes from now I would walk up to the terminal and find the driver holding a sign with the number "12" on it. I was to go with him, where I was going, I did not know. I was embarking on an adventure, surrendering to strangers.

As instructed, I put my car key in the center console and locked the doors. I was instructed that I needed nothing but the clothes on my back, my wallet with ID, social security card and the envelope of cash, so I didn't have a bag. I walked down to the terminal and there in front of a limo was a man holding a sign that said "Welcome, Twelve." The letters were in calligraphy text type and the word 'Twelve' was spelled out, rather than using digits. That had made an impression on me, actually. I went to him and as he saw me approach, he lowered the sign and opened the passenger side rear door for me. I just got into the car. No hesitation. Totally stupid of me. But that is what I did. The man closed the door behind me. He went around and got in the car and off we went.

Inside the car the divider screen between the driver and the rear passenger compartment was up. There was a couple bottles of water and an assortment of crackers and cheeses on a tray in front of me, and a small display. Once we cleared the airport and were out on the street headed to the highway the display came to life. There was a beautiful woman's face looking right at me. She had dark hair pulled back loosely, into a ponytail. Her lips were bright red and glossy. She began to speak. "Hello, I am Mistress Laura. Brave of you to take this journey, Twelve. Are you comfortable?" she was smiling. "Yes" I said. She gave a small and comforting laugh. "Good. Enjoy that. You should be here in an hour or so. I will meet you." While she said that, she winked at me. "Oh, I need you to put the envelope of money and your wallet on the seat next to you and leave them there when you get out of the car. We will take care of everything for you after that." She winked again. "You will be delighted with our program. If you work at it, it will work for you. I am going to play the orientation video for you now while you ride. Again, welcome Twelve." Her voice was silky and provocative. She smiled and the screen went blank. I put my wallet and the cash on the seat next to me as she told me to and then the screen came to life again. There was soft orchestra music playing and the images on the screen were of smiling women. It was showing them laughing with other women, different women in all sorts of environments. Alternating between the mall, at a table in a restaurant, on a beach, in a living room. Just normal looking women in all sorts of places who looked happy. "Welcome to your future. It's female." A voice said. I recognized the voice to be Mistress Raven's. "Today you start your personal journey of commitment to women. You can be proud of yourself. You will be in good company, too. There have been many men before you to abandon their "Macho" ways in favor of serving a woman properly and making women happy. You will learn how to honor women. You will become an expert at pleasing women. The mistakes that society has instilled in men for thousands of years will be erased from you and you will begin your new fulfilling life in service to women. This will be an enormous transformation for you, and it likely will not happen quickly. The male ego doesn't break easily. But break it will. Your training might at times be painful, it will be painful, but, no pain…….no gain. No matter if you were referred to us by your wife or girlfriend, or if you are among the special and rare men who apply on their own, we promise you will be transformed into what you should have always been. What nature intended you to be in the first place. You will have a daily ritual of obedience training, endurance training, sex education, manners and serving techniques and positions training. Proper hygiene, time management training. Diet and exercise. And much, much more. We cannot tell you how long this will take. We only promise that you will not graduate before you are ready. We one hundred percent guarantee your transformation. Before you are returned to your wife, or girlfriend. We will ensure that you will be acceptable to them. If you are found not to be acceptable or in the case of self-applicants, we have a placement program we are proud of. We are also proud of our 'zero failure' rate. And you will notice the pride we take in our mission to change the world, one man at a time." The music continued and the images continued, but the narration had stopped. I just felt a little scared. I had always known I was a submissive man. I remember being excited as a child when cat woman tied up and tortured batman. Or when Gomez was flirted with by his wife on the Adams family. I didn't know what it was about it then, but I knew it was something. I remember my mother's disappointment when she put her foot down about something, my dad ignored her. I never wanted to be like him. I truly admired and was excited by strong women taking charge.

Before too long we arrived. The driver turned the limo onto a driveway and stopped at the gate. Without even pushing a button, the gate opened, and we drove inside the gate. There was a white sign that said "Renovation" in large block red letters. I could see several large red brick buildings, two of them were 3 stories tall. White framed windows, there was a stone archway over the obvious entrance and steps up to a concrete pad in front of the double entry doors. There were some Latin words on the arch that were carved into the stone. Big roman looking letters.

The car stopped, and the doors unlocked. I took the hint and got out of the car. Once I closed the door, the car left, heading back down the drive towards the gate it had just came thru. I stood there looking at the building. Very nice one too. Upon closer inspection, I saw the steps and the platform were marble. It looked old, weathered, but in perfect condition. Well maintained. The landscaping was beautiful as well, rose bushes every 3 feet in the front from end to end.

I was wondering what I should do, if I should enter the building or wait where I was. While I was trying to make up my mind, one of the doors opened and out walked a very short woman dressed in white button up long sleeve blouse that had lace on the collar and the cuffs. Each button was buttoned. She was wearing a black skirt and black high heels that were so shiny the sun light beamed off them like mirrors. I recognized her as Mistress Laura. She stopped at the top step and looked down onto me from there. "You have arrived. Take off all of your clothes including your shoes, fold them neatly and put your shoes on top, then hold the stack in front of you." She produced a chrome stopwatch in her hand and depressed the button starting the clock ticking. I began doing as she asked, feeling embarrassed at being nude in front of this woman I did not know. The air was cool on my skin and the sunshine was warming it all at the same time. I was so pale, I remember thinking. When I had finished, she stopped the clock, looked at it, and shook her head. "Now on your knees, climb these steps and bring that pile of rags inside." And she started the clock again. I found that task to be very hard to do without my hands. When I made it to the top and headed for the door she turned and walked in front of me, opening the door. She stood aside and as I entered, she stepped to the side, and closed the door behind me. Then she stopped the clock. The floors were a very polished dark hard wood, and my knees were thankful. We were standing inside a foyer that was nicely decorated. The walls were pink, and the ceiling, base boards and door casings were white. There wasn't a sound that I could hear. Everything was quiet. She started walking down a long hall that was full of doors, and stopped ten feet in. She pulled opened a brass compartment door in the wall that said "Waste" engraved into the polished brass cover. "Put those rags in here" she told me, holding it open for me. "You will never need them again." She smiled at me waiting for me to comply. When I smiled back at her, the smile left her face instantly, and it was replaced with a look of scorn, maybe hate. Disgust. It was a very mean look and she sold it completely. I began to move towards her on my knees. I put my pile of folded clothes, and my shoes, in the trash chute, reportedly never to be seen again. The idea of never needing my clothes again scared me a little. The image of how the Jews were stripped of their clothes before being led into the gas chambers briefly entered my mind. I also was feeling embarrassed and was surprised to see that I was developing an erection. Mistress Laura noticed it too, and she made her displeasure known with an audible huff. She turned and proceeded down the long hallway. I followed her on my hands and knees without being told. She came to the first of many doors on the long hall and stopped to wait for me to catch up, tapping her foot with her arms folded in front of her. She had a look of impatience on her face. I sped up the best that I could, but hands and knees wasn't a familiar position to me, and I did feel clumsy. Plus, my knees were hurting already. I looked up at her face, and as I was passing through the door into the large room, she brought her foot up sharply and directly onto my balls. The pain was so intense, so unexpected, I fell onto my chest and my chin. "Don't you ever look up at me again!" she shouted at me. Just like that, my training began. She took the hair on the back of my head in her hand and pulled me alongside of her into the center of the room where there was a pillory. It was low to the floor, and I was still on my knees as she put my head and then my hands into it and closed it around me and locked the damned thing. She ordered me to keep my legs spread. So that's what I did.

She smoothly attached something else to my ankles, whatever it was I don't know, but it spread my legs to their limit. Literally my hips, and even my knee joints, ached instantly from the amount of pressure put on them being spread that wide. Soon I started moaning from the pain. I tried to look around but other than white framed windows to the outside, I couldn't see anything though my teared-up eyes. Mistress Laura was still there. She was attaching something to my balls. She stood behind me for a few minutes. Whatever it was that she attached to my balls felt like a string or something. "Female supremacy is a gift. I will require two things from you, effort and gratitude. Without your effort, this becomes a waste of time for me. Without your gratitude, this becomes a waste of time for you. Is that clear to you, Twelve?" she had not moved from behind me while she spoke. I answered "yes" and as soon as my mouth closed, she kicked me in the balls again. I screamed in pain. "You will refer to me as Mistress, is that clear?" she shouted at me in anger. "Yes Mistress!" I answered urgently, desperate for her to not hurt my balls again. "I bet it is clear, you pathetic piece of shit. I bet you think you understand, but you surely don't. Not yet. But you will, Twelve. You will understand very clearly in every fiber of your body. Repeat after me. Female supremacy is a gift." I repeated her words instantly. "Female supremacy is a gift, Mistress!". After I said that she walked around in front of me where I could see her. "It is my job to teach you. I want you to know, I love my job. I love removing a man's pride, his ego, and rebuilding him the way he should be. The way nature intended him to be. This will be hardest on you, of course, but I want you to know that for all of your suffering, there is a reward. Yes, there will be suffering. Say it again for me, Twelve." I repeated it again "Female supremacy is a gift, Mistress." She walked behind me again. She pulled on whatever was attached to my balls, I felt it tighten and there was a sharp pain followed by a dull ache. "I should just cut these balls off right now, it would make my job a lot easier. Do you agree, Twelve?" she seemed to be amused that I was in pain. I answered right away "NO, Mistress!" I started to panic. I didn't really think she would cut off my balls, but there were so many surprises so far and she seemed indifferent about my pain. Something told me she would love to do it. She hit me hard across the back side of my thighs with a long stick of some kind. "I want you to beg me to cut your balls off!" she screamed at me. I hesitated for only a moment and when I did, she brought that stick back down even harder in the same exact space. I screamed in pain and there was an immediate repeat of the strike, again in the same exact spot, "please don't cut off my balls, Mistress!" I shouted so quickly it sounded like one word. My face was wet with my tears and my entire body was on fire with pain. "I could if I wanted to, Twelve. If I owned you that is exactly what I would do, too. A man's problems begin right there in his balls. I would be doing you a favor, believe me. It would however be wrong to deprive your eventual owner of the pleasure and might surely affect your sell price. You will leave this place unmarked, intact, and well trained. Your suffering is the price you will pay for keeping your testicles. Is that understood, Twelve?" I answered, "Yes Mistress".

"Today, and today only, I will allow you to ask me questions. Not for free, understand, you will pay for each question. I cannot stand a man asking questions. But, because you are new, I will indulge you. But only for today so get them all out of your system today. You have time, it will be a long day. I expect you have at least one question right now, don't you Twelve." I honestly had a dozen questions, but out of fear, and I mean literal fear of being hurt or castrated or who knows what evil thing she would do to me. I only shook my head no. She straddled me and sat down on my back; she stroked the hair on my head. She wasn't heavy but being in the position I was in her weight was put on my throat and my hips were about to break. "Well okay, but after today, I will not tolerate any questions. You are going to learn that they are disrespectful. You will learn to listen, think, and anticipate. You will learn to have answers, not questions." Then she got up from my back, and I softly sighed with relief. She laughed loudly and hit me across my ass with the rod. It hurt so bad that it felt like it was glowing hot steel branding me. Then she rubbed her hands all over my ass and thighs where she had hit me. Her soft touch was so soothing. Then I heard her walk away and I heard the door close behind her. I could hear her heels walk away down the hall.

Whatever was attached to my balls was killing me. My balls felt like they were on fire. There I was. Left there like that in agony for what felt like hours. I had started to cry at one point. I moaned. I cried out for help. I begged please. Out the window I saw a man pass by, totally nude except for a harness that had a two-wheel cart that he was pulling attached to it. He had a harness on his head and bit in his mouth. Riding in the cart was a woman holding a whip and she whipped him as he pulled the cart as fast as he could go. Then they were gone. Then nothing. I guess I fell asleep because I didn't hear anyone enter the room, but Mistress Laura was standing in front of me again. She bent down and unlocked the pillory, then she unlocked my ankles. "Stand up" she said. I did as she said and it wasn't easy, but it felt so good. She leaned down and removed the wretched thing that was on my balls. I could only see it for a second and it looked like a very small stainless-steel cable. "Any questions for me, Twelve?" she asked looking me in the eyes. I only shook my head no, looking down to the floor. "Okay. Follow me, Twelve." She headed for the door and when I started to follow, she stopped, turned, balled her fist up and quickly hit me in my balls with her fist. I reacted by bending and turning away from her. She started screaming "ON YOUR GODDAMNED KNEES!!!! YOU STUPID PIECE OF SHIT!!! WHAT THE FUCK IS YOUR PROBLEM!!!??" I fell to my hands and knees. Doing that also caused me pain. She bent down and grabbed me by the ear and twisted it "You walk on your hands and knees. You do not walk or stand unless you are told to. Now follow me." She said softly into my ear. She let go of my ear and held the door open for me.

There were women all over the place now. Some were standing and talking, some moving down the hall. Going from room to room. Most of them were dressed in what I would call normal office attire. They were all looking at me crawl nude behind

Mistress Laura. "You have a new one, that's fun!" one of the women said as we passed. She bent down and with her bare hand slapped my ass hard. "Nice haunches" she said. Another woman pulled my hair, and another one stuck her fingers in my mouth and pulled my cheek. There was laughter, banter I couldn't make out. A few of the women followed behind me and watched me crawl along. We came to a doorway with an open door, and I saw inside there were tables and chairs inside. It looked like a big lunchroom or something. The tables were large and round. There were a few women in the room already. Some held drinks. Coffee cups, soda, iced tea was set up on a table near another door. There were sandwiches, plates of cookies. Mistress Laura walked over to a table kind of in the center of the room and put her finger in the center of it and shot a look at me. I moved across the room toward the table "up here, on all fours." I did as I was instructed. My face was beet red with embarrassment. I have never been in a room with this many women before, much less nude in front of this many people, people I didn't know. Who were they? What the hell is going on? Just then my questions got answered.

"Ladies. This is Twelve. Observe him." Mistress Laura used one pinky in my nostril to turn me on the table to face another direction, walking me around on my hands and knees in the same spot the round table for them to see me. "He has been here for 3 hours, and we have not even taught him anything yet. I simply initiated my authority to him, and he will do what I say. Once trained, he will become an excellent male. He will be ready to serve whoever gets him. Unlike the 'males' you ladies have brought here today, Twelve surrendered himself to us. He paid the same deposit you ladies paid for your 'males'. This is the reason I have him up here. You see, he had already taken the hardest step, and he did it all on his own. He accepted his reality. Your males may not fully accept it yet, but they will. Although they may need more breaking than Twelve does, they will receive the same training that Twelve will. We stand by our guarantee. You will be satisfied with your male upon graduation, or you do not have to take delivery of him, and if you choose not to continue, we will refund the tuition, and place him with a new owner. We hope that you will take advantage of the weekly owner's orientation seminar, happening right here the same time every week. Each week we will have a male, or maybe two or three, here on display to instruct you on how to maintain his training once he graduates. We will discuss some of our training methods used to that point. During that day before or after the seminar, you will be afforded the opportunity to spend time with your male, or any male you might rather spend time with. It is your choice."

Mistress Laura ran her hand down my back from my neck to my ass as she spoke and walked around the table. When she was behind me, she gently took my balls in her left hand. She held them gently, but firmly as she continued. "It is your choice" she repeated. "Get used to that. It is what nature intended. If you look here in my left hand, you can see exactly where the problems of the world originate. These testicles may come in different shapes and sizes. They may be brown or black. They all do the same thing. Cause problems. Once the male has served his natural purpose of procreation, these testicles simply are more problems than they are worth." She began pulling down on my balls as she spoke. Despite myself I was getting an erection. She was scaring me. Disturbing me. I was having vivid frightening thoughts of crazed women and mass male castration. "But we love them for these testicles. These testicles are the reason for the training. They can also be the solution. Using the testicles to control your male is a saner option than removing the testicles. We can keep them for what we like about them, and by learning how to use them we can love the testicles because thru them we have our ability to control the male. Males are much simpler than we are, but don't make the mistake in thinking they are simple. Stupid? Absolutely! Pigs? To be sure, they are!" She let go of my balls, and she gave them a slap with her hand. I felt it in my face and in my eyes. I couldn't help but yelp. She walked over and pushed my head down to the table firmly but slowly until I did it on my own. "Elbows" she said lowly to me, and I took my position. "But they have emotional problems. Just as many emotions come from those testicles as we have. But for ten thousand years men have been taught, by other men by the way, they have been taught incorrectly how to interpret them. They usually don't even recognize they are having an emotion. Only by stripping a male's pride and destroying his ego, leaving him in desperation. Forcing the rewiring of his brain to accept the emotions. Once the brain has done this, he can be in tune with you. In harmony with nature. As women, it is natural for us to be attracted to these testicles and the men who walk around with them. What is unnatural is for women to be submissive to them. So, plan to be here each week. I strongly recommend this training for you too." Mistress Laura walked back behind me, took my cock in her hand and gave it a few quick strokes. "Today I am going to instruct you all how a male is controlled, and the simple easy things you should do to insure he remains submissive to you. Males are full of desire, like I said, they are extremely emotional. They are hard wired to ejaculate. It is, really, as simple as that. The misconception that they are hard wired to copulate is just patently wrong. That is why they masturbate. All the time. Even when they aren't touching themselves, they are constantly mentally masturbating. When they get an extra minute, or when the pressure gets too much, they complete the act physically. Jacking off, sex with a partner, doesn't matter, same result. So, by controlling simply that, you begin to take control of them. Before, they themselves were in control of ejaculation. You tried to control them by not having sex with them, but that only worked a little, as soon as you did let them fuck you, it was right back to the same behavior as before. Right?" there were many women who shouted "RIGHT!" or "YES!". There was clapping and laughing too. Mistress Laura let go of my cock, which was rock hard. "Roll over" she told me.

I did as she asked, my legs dangling off the edge of the round table. Now my dick pointed up at the ceiling. I had my hands at my side. That didn't feel right, so I moved them across my chest. Mistress

Laura took my hand and put it on top of my head. I moved my other hand up there. Even though I was laying naked on a table in the center of a room full of clothed women, my cock was at full staff. I was still embarrassed, but I was accepting it. "So, we need to control his ejaculations first. This is almost impossible without a chastity cage. There are so many types and materials it will make your head spin. There are also piercings you can have done. Some devices require a piercing. But they are all usually quite effective. Simply going to be your choice. Your male will be wearing one before the end of the day today, and for his entire stay with us. If you choose to, we can simply leave it on him when you accept him back. There is an additional charge, but he will already be accustomed to wearing the one we use here. We use the Bon4 stainless steel cage here, on all of our males. We have found it to be very durable and hygienic. By the end of our time together today, you will see me show you how to put it on Twelve here. But first..." my erection had started to falter, and she reached over and stroked my cock slowly a couple of times, until it had regained its stature. "First, let's talk about orgasms." Mistress Laura let go of my cock and there were giggles throughout the room. My cock twitched a few times causing more giggles. "Males orgasm in different ways, they also ejaculate in different ways. I can make poor Twelve here orgasm without an ejaculation and I can make him ejaculate without having an orgasm. Both are necessary."

She stopped doing anything at all. She stopped talking. She just stood there looking down at my cock. When I cocked my head to see her face better, she made eye contact with me, and I instantly knew I had fucked up. Before I could even break eye contact, she had made a fist and punched me in the balls again. I swear it felt like I had been electrocuted. My eyes saw white and then stars, and I was blinded for a moment. I had moved my hands from my head and covered my cock and balls, my erection completely gone. She had moved around the table too. Taking a fist full of my hair and pulling hard, I became aware of her screaming face only an inch from mine. "YOU DON'T LOOK AT MY FACE UNLESS I TELL YOU

TOO!! THIS IS NOT FOR YOUR PLEASURE! I DO NOT *OWE* YOU ANY PLEASURE!" She literally pulled me off the table and onto the floor by my hair. I lay there and I was crying, curled up in a ball. "Get on your knees, NOW! Get out of my face. Wait for me in the hallway" She walked over and opened the door, holding it for me. I made my way out the doorway and she used her foot to push me down by my ass. "Stay there."

The laughter from both the inside of the room and from the women in the hallway filled my ears. I was sobbing but trying to pull myself together. The laughter died down a bit, I could hear mistress Laura talking, but not what she was saying. One of the women in the hallway shouted at me "Hang in there, boy. It is worth it." I was feeling quite a bit of pain from my groin. My knees were bruised from walking on them. Where she pulled my hair felt like ants were biting me. Now women were just walking by me, around me, over me like I wasn't there. The giggles continued but weren't loud or as frequent. The floor was cold, and it made me ache worse.

I am sure I was in that predicament for at least thirty minutes when the door opened and snickering women streamed out the doorway, stepping over me. They headed towards the entrance, talking to each other. I heard one of them say "awe. Boo. Boo. Boo. Poor baby." With a sarcastic tone. Then mistress Laura was in front of me. "On your knees, 12." Her voice not harsh or cruel. I did as she asked, raising myself to my hands and knees, keeping my eyes low. "Sit on your heels, 12. Face me." I kept my eyes low still after doing what she asked.

She crouched down to my level and brought her hand to my face and wiped my tears away. She lifted my face by my chin. Her expression was soft, caring. She looked sorry for me. She lifted me by my chin as she said softly to me "Stand up, 12." As I rose, I became aware of pain again and I guess I moaned because she commented. "Oh, I bet you are sore." Standing there in the hallway facing her, she took my hand and led me back into the room where the women had been. She led me back to the table I had been pulled from by my hair, but now she pulled out a chair for me and asked me to "Sit down, please." Again, in the soft voice. She brought over a pitcher of water and 2 glasses, filled them both up and gave me one. Then she sat across the table from me.

"Are you hurt? Would you like medical attention, 12?"

"No, Mistress." I replied. She smiled at me.

"You will always be cared for, 12. Even if it might not seem like you are. Your health is every bit as important as is your training. So, you should tell me if you need medical. Do you understand?"

I nodded my head that I understood. The next thing I knew she was standing behind me with her hands around my throat. She squeezed my throat very hard, and in a low, controlled, but very angry voice she said to my ear "You are to verbally respond anytime a woman, ANY WOMAN, asks you a question. Nodding your head is very, VERY disrespectful!" I began to choke, but she didn't let go. She held on to my throat with both hands and continued. "you're going to learn some manners!" I started to have a hard time breathing and she let go of my throat just in time. I thought I was about to pass out. I honestly was just glad she wasn't punching my balls or pulling my hair. Seriously. "Did I make myself clear to you, you repugnant sorry excuse for a man? Did I reach your pea sized brain?" her voice was filled with vile disgust, but she wasn't screaming. I quickly responded, verbally this time, "Yes Mistress! I'm sorry Mistress! It will never happen again, Mistress!" I meant every word. I truly did.

"I hope not, 12. Because I am going to go ahead and make you a promise. I will make sure you will regret it for the rest of your life. You will never be able to forget what I will do to you. I mean exactly what I say, and I hope you take me seriously." I did take her seriously. I thought she was wildly overreacting, but I took her seriously.

She walked back over and got her glass of water, took a drink and sat back down across from me. "Right now, 12, we are going to have a conversation. I want you to simply be honest. I said before

I will only allow your questions today and today only. I am also going to let you know what you are in for, in case you haven't figured it out yet, this is not going to be easy for you. I want you to listen first, then ask your questions." She tapped on the table a couple of times. She got up from the table and walked over to the door, opened it and told someone in a low voice "I am ready now." Then she closed the door and returned to where she was sitting at the table. "I had planned to shave your head, 12. Just like every other male here. But your hair is so beautiful, and it seems to be helpful to getting your attention, so I have decided to let you keep it. However, you will wear a chastity cage like every other male here. There will be an adjustment period where your body will try to reject it. It will at times become painful. But you will wear it, nonetheless. I want you to understand that you are wearing it for me, and for your eventual owner. I may remove it anytime I wish. But no other person can. If you remove it, oh, and that would be a tragic mistake, measures will be taken that neither you nor I wish to happen."

The door opened and a man walked in holding a tray in both hands. Behind him followed a blond woman dressed in a black pantsuit she held a black leather bag in one hand, but it wasn't a purse. It was like a doctor's bag you might see on tv. I had never seen one in person before.

The nude man set the tray down in front of me on the table. On the tray was a covered dish, a glass of iced tea, some flat wear, and a couple of napkins. He then took 2 steps back behind me, knelt down on his knees, looking at the floor. I did notice the metal cage on his penis.

"Eat, 12." My Mistress said to me. I responded, verbally, clearly "Yes Mistress. Thank you, Mistress." I was quite hungry. Then I removed the cover and saw the pile of whatever it was on the plate. It looked as if it had already been eaten. I just stared at it. I didn't know what it was. Or once was. Clearly it had come out of a blender. I had never been served anything as gross looking as this was. There wasn't a great amount of it. Looked like about two ice cream scoops worth. I could see some lettuce, a piece of tomato. I made out a couple of sesame seeds in the mix of brown and swirled white piled up mess. I was still looking at it motionless when I heard my mistress ask "12, what's wrong? I know that there isn't very much, it is only half a hamburger and there is no cheese. But you start your diet today. You are going to lose some of that extra weight you are carrying." I just looked at it still and then she asked me "what's wrong, 12? Eat your hamburger." I felt like I was going to be sick "mistress…I…. I don't…." I managed to say. "Is there something wrong with it?" she asked firmly "you don't like it?" she rose from her seat and walked around beside me. "No mistress. I don't like this." She walked over to the nude man who was still kneeling "What did you do to mess up his dinner?" she slapped the man across his face, but he held his position. "Mistress, I prepared his the same as the others" he answered calmly even as he recovered from the slap. "Well, he doesn't seem to like it. You must have messed it up somehow." She walked over to where I was sitting at the table and stood over me. I now had the fork in my hand and was in the process of getting a bit of what I would call slop. She picked up the plate and examined it. "It does look a little funny. Too much mayonnaise maybe?" then she set the plate back down in front of me again. She walked smoothly over to another table against the wall and picked up a leather strap that had a wood handle. Turning around looked at the man kneeling. "PRESENT!" she shouted at him, and he fell forward on his elbows. She lowered the strap across his ass 5 times in rapid hard blows. The man did not make a sound, nor move from his position even a fraction of an inch. "I expected better of you. This is unacceptable." Then she released another flurry of assault on his haunches. Still, he remained in position, but I did hear him whimper as she struck him at least 10 more times. Hoping she might stop I scooped a fork full in my mouth. Then another. It didn't taste bad at all, actually. It tasted like a hamburger with a bit too much mayonnaise. When I took my third bite, she stopped beating him and turned her attention to me. I was about half done eating it. "Oh. You can eat it, I see. What the hell is this shit?!!" she left the man and walked over to me and grabbed my hair again. She pulled my head back by my hair and looked me in the eye. "So, there is nothing wrong with it?" I swallowed what was in my mouth and said "No, Mistress. No. No. Nothing." I stumbled out in agony from my hair being pulled again. "So, you were lying then. Testing me. Get on your knees and present!" She shouted at me in obvious anger, letting go of my hair. Once I was on my knees, she laid that strap across my ass in a crooked line that also struck the top of my right thigh and lower ass as well as the upper ass cheek. Then she did it again in the same exact spot which was in excruciating pain. I lost my position as I, involuntarily mind you, tried to escape the punishment. Involuntarily or not, my Mistress definitely did not take kindly towards the action. She swooped down and grabbed my hair pulling my head upward harshly. "HOLD YOUR POSITION, WORM!!! Don't try to WORM your way away from me! You have a beating coming your way now! "She then started to hit me with the strap, very hard, over and over. I don't know how many times. I started crying. Sobbing, really. My entire body was a big hurt. My head felt like I had been scalped. My knees felt like I was in a car wreck. My ass was on fire and just one big hurt. Each strike caused me to involuntarily jolt and trying to stay still I pulled back against each jolt. I was literally rocking back and forth, and that is when I noticed I had an erection. I could feel my cock and balls swinging while she belted away at my posterior. Suddenly she stopped. I was still sobbing from the pain, but she just stood there. Minutes went by before my sobbing was controllable. "Since you insist on displaying the manners of an animal, Twelve, you can eat like one now." She grabbed my unfinished plate from the table and set it in front of me on the floor, removing the fork of course.

"EAT!" She shouted, simultaneously the strap landed on my ass again. But only once. Once was plenty. I pushed my face down into the slop and sucked it in, lapped it in, and licked the plate clean in a matter of seconds. I was sobbing the whole time. I didn't think I could take anymore abuse.

"There now I guess it isn't that bad after all. Stand up and put your hands on your head. Your manners are going to improve, 12. I personally guarantee it." I stood and painfully raised my hands to my head which also hurt. She walked back to her seat at the table, set down her strap and picked up her glass of water. She took a drink and set the glass back down. "Just stand there, 12." Her voice was cold and mean. My eyes, stinging wet with tears, were focused on a spot on the floor. A gun shot in the room could not have caused me to raise my eyes. I was aware of the blond woman holding the black bag just standing off to the side, and of the nude man down on his hands and knees. But I wasn't going to look at them. Mistress Laura sat there quietly for a few minutes looking at me. When you are standing nude in front of strangers with your hands on your head, you really get a sense for how long a minute is. After what felt like an hour Mistress Laura spoke softly. "Slave, you may rise. Collect the dishes and return to your duties. Mistress Brooke, we are ready for what you have for us." The man rose and did as he was told, collecting the plate from the floor along with the remaining silverware from the table and put it all back on the tray and then exited the room. Upon the door closing behind him Mistress Brooke walked slowly over and set the black bag on the table. Without a word she opened it and produced a blind fold and walked over to me. "Lower your arms." She said in a very high-pitched voice. I did as I was told and she put the blindfold over my eyes, sending me into darkness. I heard her return to her bag and rummage thru it. Or perhaps she emptied it out, it was hard to tell. I felt her grab my cock and she pulled me over to the table. "Bend over and put your hands flat on the chair" she said, her voice sounding sweet and chipper. She guided my hands where she wanted them and put them flat. "And spread your legs as wide as they will go." I complied. I was so sore bending with my legs spread was painful, but I kept the pain to myself. I did not want any more torment, that was for sure.

I could smell the alcohol as she put it on a cotton ball. She swabbed a large area on my right ass cheek. She put energy into it, scrubbing the area very good. Then came a needle into my ass cheek and I felt the injection. I wondered what it was, but I was left wondering. I could feel the substance numbing my ass. It felt weird, but the ache disappeared. I was so thankful. She applied a band aid. Then I could feel the numbness spread. She was wiping my ass cheeks with a damp towel, even getting in between them and wiping my anus. It wasn't a caring loving or sensual type of cleansing. More like somebody cleaning a stovetop or something, but I could feel how numb I was getting. When she used a fresh towel to clean my groin, my cock and my balls I couldn't feel a thing. I could smell the shave cream before she covered my scrotum with it. She smothered my perineum completely and proceeded to shave me. I suddenly got scared as she was shaving my balls. I feared she was preparing my balls to be cut off. Thankfully that did not turn out to be the case. She went about what she was doing in an expert manner. I felt none of it. I could feel pressure when she grabbed my balls in her hand and pulled them. She dried my lower half with a towel. Then I felt her rubbing my balls and my cock. She worked my balls for a few moments. Then I could hear something metallic being put on the table, it sounded a little bit like silverware tinkling against each other. That's when I realized I was being fitted with a chastity device. "Stand up straight, put your hands-on top of your head." She told me. I did exactly as she asked. She installed the cage with no issues, and I heard the lock close with a click. She pulled on the cage, and I could feel the pressure around my balls. I could sense the weight of the cage.

The blindfold was removed, and my eyes squinted to see in the bright light. Mistress Laura was sitting at the table. She had both hands on of the table. The leather strap she used to beat me with sitting there. She smiled. I avoided eye contact, fearing another beating. Mistress Brooke walked over to her and handed her 2 keys, presumably to the lock that now secured the cage shrouding my cock and cupping my balls. She reached into her shirt and clipped the keys to a chain she was wearing. The keys dangled there between her breasts. "12, Thank Mistress Brooke for her efforts on your behalf." Mistress Laura said. I immediately replied, "Thank you Mistress Brooke, thank you for doing this for me." I stood there not looking at her and she simply said, "you are very welcome, 12." In her high, and cheerful voice.

"Okay, we are done here. Come with me now, 12." She said and rose from the table, grabbing the strap, and headed for the door. I went down to my knees and turned to follow her. I felt better. I could feel the swinging of my penis, and the prison it was in, as I managed to move my legs. The pain was gone from my ass, and even my sore knees didn't feel so sore now. She held open the door and I smoothly made my way thru it. She took me down the hall and out the front door we had entered thru what seemed to me like a day ago. As she promised, it had been a long day. It was just about dark now. I saw a woman using a water hose to wash a man on all fours in front of another building. I could see he had a cage on his cock too. His head was shaved, and he looked rather unhappy. She was making it a priority to point the stream of the water in his face. We crossed past them to the building behind them. We entered in the front thru a door made of highly varnished wood. Inside the door there was a rug covering a wood floor. Mistress Laura closed the door behind me. "This is where we live, 12. Welcome home. Wait right here for me." And with that she entered a room to the right. The room was a large foyer attached to a sitting room on my left. There was a long hallway, and I could see that there was a staircase halfway down the hall. She returned after only a couple of minutes. Without even a word proceeded down the hall. I followed close and before we reached the stairs, she opened a door on the right side of the hallway. As she held the door open for me, I entered. It was a large apartment. There was a modern living room carpeted in shag carpet. I saw a kitchen, dining room, and a couple of doors on both sides of the living room. I was excited about the carpet. There was a large tv in the living room. It was decorated with a woman's touch, but not what I would have called girly. She set down the strap on a table next to the sofa.

"Stand up, 12." She said. I did, but with some difficulty. "Oh, poor baby. I know you must be sore; you've had a long day!" she said let me give you the tour, this will be your home for…. A while." She took me by the hand into the kitchen, opened a few cabinets, the fridge, she didn't say a word, and then led me into the bedroom. It was very large. It had a king-sized bed and there were a pair of doors that met in the middle opening into a large bathroom. There was a large garden whirlpool tub and next to it was a big shower stall with a bench that you could get 4 people into. There was a large double sink lavatory counter and a mirror the full width of it. That's when I got the first glimpse of myself. All my pubic hair was removed and my prisoner penis with its shiny steel prison. I stared at my reflection in the mirror. "You are going to get used to it." She said as she put her arms around me and caressed my back. She put her head on my chest and looked at the reflection of us together in the mirror. I just instinctually put my arms around her to and we stood there like that for a moment or two. She broke off the embrace and simply said "run a bath" and she left the room. I started the tub filling with water, and then I had to pee, so I went to the toilet, lifted the seat and started to pee into the toilet. This was the first time I touched the cage. I caressed my sore balls and felt how tight they felt in the cage. It was a new sensation I had never had before. Once I finished peeing, I flushed the toilet and lowered the seat again.

"Get in the tub, 12" she said. I had not realized she was standing in the doorway, so I was a bit startled. She laughed out loud at that. "Calm down, boy. Just try to relax, get in the tub. Let's let the stress of today evaporate, and we can soothe your body a bit." Her voice was sweet and comforting. I went over and stepped into the tub and sat down. "You may feel free to use my toilet when you need to, 12. Also there is another one you may use on the other side of the apartment. But I expect you to sit down. Standing up to pee is not allowed any more, and I will punish you the next time I see, or hear you, doing that. That is a privilege for real men.

Not submissive men such as yourself. Is that clear?" her voice was still sweet and comforting. "Yes Mistress." I answered obediently. "Good, 12. Good boy." I felt shame. But also, I felt my cock twitch against the cage. She reached into a cabinet and produced some pink bath salts. She sprinkled a generous amount of the salts in the tub around me as the water was now covering my legs. It did feel soothing. When the water was high enough, she turned on the whirlpool and shut off the faucet. The water jetted out around me, and bubbles rose up and a white soapy foam covered the top. "Lean back and relax, 12. Just take in the bubbles and think about today's lessons. I want you to know that you did very well, and that I am proud of you. Good boy." And then she patted me on the head, then left me there to soak.

I did exactly as she asked, and soon I fell asleep. She woke me up gently, giggled, and turned off the tub. She was wearing a red knee length night gown and white fluffy slippers. "Okay, sleepy. Reach down there and pull the drain stopper up and climb out of there." She reached around behind her and grabbed a towel. I stood up and she draped the towel around my shoulders and said "Dry yourself off" I was doing that, and she laid another towel down on the floor for me to step on and as she reached out her hand, I took her hand and stepped out of the tub. I dried myself off the rest of the way. She took the towel away from me and dried my prisoner penis better. Her hands holding my balls up as she dried my perineum felt amazing and I just stood there. For the first time that day I felt cared for.

She moved to the vanity, opened a drawer and pulled out a hair dryer. "Come over here, 12." And I did as she asked facing her while she plugged the hair dryer in and proceeded to use it to dry my prisoner penis completely. It felt good at first but then the steel began to heat up and that felt terrible. She stopped when she was satisfied that I was dry. Setting the hair dryer down she picked up a tube of something and squirted a bit into her hand. Using her other hand, she spread the cream on me around the ring and all over my balls. It felt amazing. Cooling my skin all over. Then she washed her hands in the sink and dried them off with a towel. She turned and headed for the door, then stopped and looked at me. "Come with me." She said. I dropped to my knees and followed her into the bedroom. She sat on the edge of the bed, which already had the covers pulled back. She pointed at a spot between her feet that were not touching the floor. As I crawled to the spot, she grabbed my hair and pulled my head between her thighs. At the same time, she laid backwards raising her sex to my face. I felt light-headed. Her aroma was strong. Her vagina was wet, and I took to licking softly between the folds. Pushing my tongue into her opening, I tasted her essence. I could feel her pulse on my tongue as I licked up to her clit, which was stiff. When my tongue passed over her clit the first time, I felt her convulse and shudder. She moaned loudly, with no restraint and after only a few minutes she exploded in orgasm. She became extremely wet. I made an honest attempt to lap up all her fluids, but when I came too close to her clit, she stopped me, pushed my head away. She did not say a word, she just pushed me back with her foot. She stuck her big toe of her left foot into my mouth. I licked it and sucked on it and then proceeded to lick her whole foot. I had never licked a woman's feet before. I was enjoying it, my prisoner penis making its best attempt at a jail break, but unsuccessfully. After I gave oral worship to her left foot from heel to in between each beautiful toe, she gave me her right foot to service, placing her left one on my shoulder. I gave her right foot the same exact attention too. After she tired of that she rose up on her feet directly in front of me, gave my hair a pull gently, and said "Good boy".

She stepped around me and went back into the restroom, closed the door. I remained where I was, not wanting a punishment for moving or something like that. When she returned, she went to the closet and returned with 2 blankets and a pillow. Setting the pillow and one of the blankets on the bed, she spread one of the blankets on the floor beside the bed, but towards the foot of the bed. She pointed at it and told me to lay down on it with my head towards the foot, and she put the pillow down there as she said it. I did as I was told, and she covered me up with the blanket and then got into her bed.

I laid there. Sleep eluded me as I recalled the events from the day. How she beat me, how she kicked me. I was sore from most all of it. But her scent filled my nostrils, and her taste was on my tongue, and it made me smile to myself. I felt warm and comfortable as I could hear her sleeping soundly. She was the only thing on my mind as I finally fell asleep.

The next day began with her teaching me how to begin each day. I was to fold my blankets, make her bed, and attend her in the shower. She showed me how she liked her body to be lathered up, her hair shampooed. Conditioned and rinsed. Towel dried, then blow dried. Lotion applied to her entire body. She allowed me to remain upright in the apartment, but she told me that all areas outside the apartment I was to follow her and remain on all fours. She also remained nude most of the morning as she put an apron on me and directed me to make her coffee and breakfast. She sat on a towel still nude and drank her coffee and ate her toast. She had me remove my apron and sit at her feet under the table. She reached down and stroked my hair a couple of times, pulling it occasionally. I wasn't given anything to eat or drink. I would have loved a cup of coffee, but I kept that to myself.

After having me help her get dressed we left the apartment, me following her on all fours. Today she chose to wear jeans and a tee shirt. Her breast under the tee shirt could be clearly seen as she did not wear a bra. She took me to the main building again, but this time she took me upstairs. Navigating the stairs was a new challenge and keeping up proved beyond my capability. On the second floor in the hallway, she grabbed my ear and pulled it very hard telling me rather loudly in my ear to "Keep up! Dammit!" and believe me I made every effort to do exactly that. She led me to a classroom. It looked just like a classroom out of school. She seated me at a desk in the front. There were ten other men seated at desks. All these men had their heads shaved. Also, I could see they all had chastity cages on. There was a woman standing in front of the classroom facing the school desks. She was wearing a very tight white blouse and a grey pencil skirt that was slender and fell around her mid-calf. She had on some very high heel shoes that clicked against the hardwood floor as she walked. On a chalk board behind her in large letters were the words "Why you are here".

"I am Mistress Parker. And this is day one of your education. Class starts at 10am sharp. Everyday. You will not be late. The seat you are sitting in is where you are to sit each day. Mistress Laura will be assisting me today. Other training Mistresses will be here on other days. But each of you, and of course I, will be here. Everyday. Raise your hand if you do not understand that for some reason." None of us did. "Good." She said as she walked over to a large wooden desk and picked up a long pointer rod. Moving over to the chalk board she pointed at the words smacking the board with the rod in a sharp 'smack'.

"You might think you know why you are here, and while there may be some truth in what you think, it doesn't matter. It doesn't matter what you think. What you" 'SMACK' she smacked the board again with each word "think" 'SMACK' "doesn't" 'SMACK' "Matter." 'SMACK' "that is why you are here. To learn that, and repeat after me if you know it, 'What you think doesn't matter'" the whole room repeated after her. She walked, loudly, over to a man sitting to my right and lowered the rod onto his desk and asked: "what do you think?" and he said quickly "it doesn't matter, Mistress." "That's right. It doesn't matter." She moved back to the front of the room holding the rod in both hands. "This is going very smoothly. Wonderful. The reason, or reasons, that what you think doesn't matter is a question of history and society. From now on, you will stand apart from historic societal norms and you will adopt a different convention. A new reality. A better way. Better for you, better for your Mistress, better for society and the future of the world. You have been taught that 'men' matter more than women, and what women think means less than you. You have been taught that, because women have emotions, somehow, they are less capable than men, and at the same time taught to suppress and hide your own emotions. Men have been programmed to believe this from a very young age, and society supports this lie. But it is just that. A lie. You are going to learn that: you have emotions. You are going to learn that: women are not the weaker sex. You are going to learn that: you have an obligation to serve ALL women. And you are going to learn how to do it properly." She walked right up to me, placed the rod on my desktop and said "You have too much hair. Are you special?" I answered right away "No Mistress." She removed the rod from my desktop and moved to the man sitting to the left of me. "What do you think of his hair?" and the man was confused, because he answered: "it is too long, Mistress." She brought the rod down swiftly on top of his right hand and she told him "What you think doesn't matter" she turned around and said "Get on your knees over here. Now!" pointing at the floor. The man moved, clearly upset. He was on his hands and knees with his ass facing the class. "Get down on your elbows." She told him in a very cold voice that clearly expressed her disgust. She walked up behind him and placed the rod gently on his ass cheeks. She rubbed it back and forth. "Men are stupid. It isn't your fault, really. But it is true." She tapped on his exposed scrotum with her rod repeatedly until the man was yelping. His ball sack was swollen from wearing the chastity cage. She just kept doing it. Not hard, but that didn't seem to matter because, pretty soon the man was crying. I watched in horror as she began hitting his testicles harder and harder. When she stopped, he was screaming in pain, and I could see that the skin had broken open and a small amount of blood was oozing out. "Physical pain is temporary. The amount of pain you are feeling now might be the most you have ever felt. Should I continue beating your balls? What do you think?" she asked the man who was pathetically sobbing. He painfully answered between sobs "What I think doesn't matter, Mistress!" she walked around in front of him. "That's right. It doesn't matter. Class, do you think I was too hard on his poor ball sack?" and together we answered her "What I think doesn't matter, Mistress!" She put the rod under her left armpit and began clapping her hands, sarcastically. "Very good class! Very good!"

"A man is to serve women. To serve women properly, you must give your body to them completely. You will learn how to please women in many ways. Your life now belongs to a woman, your training Mistress. Your personal training will be by her. Her rules apply inside her apartment. My rules apply in this class. Every female is over you; they are your boss. You must do what they tell you. Now we will break for lunch. All of you go downstairs to the lunchroom. After lunch we will meet outside in front of the building. Go now."

All of us began out of the room on our hands and knees. The poor man who had his balls beaten was still crying from the pain, but he made his way slowly down the stairs too. We made our way into the lunchroom, where I spent painful time the day before. As we entered the room the odor of pizza filled my nostrils. I love pizza, so it raised my spirits. That is, of course, before I saw that lunch had undergone the same treatment as supper the night before did. There was the same man who took such a beating at my stubborn refusal to eat the blended burger. I made a vow to myself to not be the reason someone else took punishment again. I felt horrible about it. He was standing, wearing a pressed white cotton apron, behind a table full of trays, each with a covered plate, a plastic fork, and a small glass of iced tea. I scanned the room and there was not a Mistress in it. Just him and the 11 of us entering on our hands and our knees. I was confused about what to do. I guess we all were because none of us did anything. We just sort of stopped and waited for a minute. The man in the apron didn't say a word, he just looked straight ahead, arms behind his back. After a few minutes Mistress Parker came into the room and told us to rise, get a tray and sit at a table and have lunch. She warned us against talking, and as we had only fifteen minutes left, we had better hurry too.

After taking my tray from the man in the apron, who made no notice of me whatsoever, I found a seat, back at the same table as the day before, and I sat down. I set down my tray, I removed the cover from the plate to find a paper plate with a single scoop of pureed pizza. My heart sank. Fifteen minutes proved to be ample time to eat it all and drink the tea. Which I did without a comment. I could have eaten everyone's portion, that is how hungry I was. Getting up, I stretched my back and returned my tray to the man in the apron. Got back on my knees and headed outside. There were a few women in the hallway on the way to the front door. They all looked at me, some whistled. As I passed by them a woman slapped me on the ass, and another pulled my hair. Eventually I made it outside and down the large marble steps, Mistress Laura was there waiting for me. The other men were close behind me. When we were all there, Mistress Laura told us to stand up and to line up facing her.

"Today we are going to learn some positions. Together. Mistress Parker will be along in a few minutes. Place your hands on your head, stand up straight, and spread your feet apart about twenty-four inches." We all did exactly that. "This is position number one. When a woman tells you 'One' or holds a single finger up on her right hand," she held up her right forefinger for us to see as she walked around checking our posture "you are immediately to assume this position facing her. She may want to inspect you. She may want to give you instructions and want your undivided attention. She may simply want you to stand where she can see you, but not be bothered by you. She may want to whip you with a bullwhip. You are to hold this position without moving until she tells you otherwise. She might leave the room, or even the building, you are to remain in the position she puts you in without moving. Even if you think she forgot about you. Even if the phone rings. Even if there is a knock at the door." She walked behind me and when she did, she caressed my ass cheeks and kept walking. "Perhaps if the house or building were on fire and your Mistress was not there, then I would move to safety after ensuring your Mistress was safe first." She walked back in front of us, looked at us all.

Then she said: "So far, so good." Then remained there looking at us before continuing "Does everybody now know position one?" we all said out loud "Yes Mistress". And she continued. "Now say you are at position one, as you are now, and your Mistress says to you 'Present', can anyone show me what you are to do?" None of the men, including myself, did or said anything. "Okay. Bend at the waist and grab your knees, or lower if you can, leaving your legs spread as they are. Do it." We all did. It is harder than it sounds after being on your knees so much. Even standing up straight with legs spread was beginning to be uncomfortable. I was bent over holding my legs below my knees and looking down at the grass. Mistress Laura was walking behind us checking our posture. "She may be showing you off to someone. She might want to spank you with a paddle. She may even be about to fuck you with a dildo. In any position you might be in, you are expected to hold that position until told or forced to change. How and where to stand or sit is no longer a choice you have. If you are not told how or where, you will do what you have been told to do in the past. The standing orders. Your Mistress's default preference. She might not give you position orders at all, ever. But she will have a way and a place she wants or likes you to be until she requires you. You are to be thinking of her, her needs, her wants. Here, you will be told what that is. You will learn what your training Mistress wants, needs. You will always strive to please her. You will learn by the numbers. One!" she said firmly. I stood back up. Put my hands back on my head. One of the men did not. He must not have been listening, whatever his problem was he now had a new one. Mistress Laura walked up behind him and grabbed his balls in her hand and pulled. I knew from experience how that felt and understood why he screamed so loud. "What is your problem? You aren't listening to me? You can't pay attention for five damn minutes? Answer me!" he yelled out "I am sorry Mistress!" repeatedly, over and over very quickly as he assumed the number one position. "I bet." She said, letting go of his balls. She walked around him to face him. "Get on your stomach, arms and legs spread out, nose to the dirt! Do it!" she wasn't yelling, but her message was loud and clear. He dropped flat on the ground just as told. "Stay there!" and then she turned and walked away from us all.

She went into the building, slamming the door behind her. After a few minutes she returned holding a leather strap, I would learn later that it was a Scottish tawse. A simply horrible instrument of pain. She was also holding something else in her hand. She walked up to the man on his stomach and kicked him in his side. "On your knees! Can you hear me? Hello?" she tormented him as he rose to his knees. Putting the tawse between her knees she then produced a blindfold. She roughly placed it over his eyes and tied it tightly behind his head. "Get your nose back in the dirt. I am going to help you to listen and to pay attention. HEAD DOWN ASS UP!!" She walked back in front of the rest of us, holding the tawse in her hand. "You all need some exercise, and I thought it would be fun to have a little contest. I want you to run around the main building, the first male back and at number one position here, wins. I am going to have a talk with this male who chooses to ignore me. I want his attention. I want you run as fast as you can, because I will reward the winner...but the last male back gets punished. Okay? Ready. Set. GO!"

We all took off running. I was not in front. I had never been a great runner. But running with the chastity cage on was a different experience. It bounced my balls left and right and up and down all at the same time. After only running for about a minute it took its toll on me, and the pain slowed me down. Other men were having problems too. A few men were hauling ass, though. I reached down with one hand and cupped my balls with it and then I was running a lot faster. I was in third place as we rounded the backside of the building. I ran as fast as I could, but a couple of these men were good runners, and I was passed up by another. I could see there were women who had materialized outside in front of the building and cheering us on. Some were heckling us. They were laughing, pointing. I poured on the speed and let go of my balls. I ignored the pain from my bouncing ball sack. I managed a second-place finish, sliding into the number one position where I had started. I was out of breath and standing with my legs spread and my hands on my head felt natural and good as I caught my breath. The women were all cheering as the last man took up his position. He was obviously upset at being the loser. Mistress Laura was clapping her hands, the tawse under her left arm. The blindfolded man was still on his knees where he was. He was not smiling. The commotion died down a little. The women gathered around to watch as Mistress Laura centered herself on the line up of men catching their breath, standing at position number one. "Okay! You all made a good effort. We have a winner." She shot a look at me and frowned, then walked up to the man who won. He was a taller man, leaner too. He had a runner's physique and I bet he runs for fun. She put her hand flat on his chest. "Who is your training Mistress?" she asked him. He was smiling and said, "Mistress Kasey, Mistress.". She turned and faced the crowd of women. A slender, tall woman walked up to Mistress Laura. Standing next to her she towered above her. "What do you call this male?" my Mistress asked her, still looking at him. "Well, I had been calling him Oscar because of his skinny little wiener." The man blushed a little. "Well Oscar here has earned a reward."

Mistress Laura looked at him and said "Okay, Oscar. You are hereby relieved for today, and Mistress Kasey will reward you, I am sure. Unless you misbehave. So. Goodbye. Leave." And she turned away from him. He went back to his hands and knees and followed his training mistress off to one of the buildings. Mistress Laura then walked up to the man who came in last. He was still quite upset, and still out of breath. "Get on your knees, face down, ass up. Now." She told him as she pointed to a spot close to the blindfolded man. He did so quickly, with no hesitation. "The rest of you get on your knees, legs spread, hands behind your backs." We were doing what she asked when she told us "This is position two" then she walked over to the two men. "Who is your training mistress, slow poke?" she asked him as she looked over at me and shook her head back and forth. "Mistress Janet." He answered in a shaky tone. Another one of the women came over to Mistress Laura from the crowd of women. She was maybe 25, medium height and weight.

Her brown hair was shoulder length and straight. I wouldn't call her 'pretty'. She was dressed in jeans and a button up plaid shirt. She was wearing sneakers. "What do you call this pathetic male, Mistress Janet?" Mistress Laura asked her smiling. "Oh, I call him 'Dogboy'." They both laughed. Still laughing as she looked at him, Mistress Laura "I like that. That's awesome. 'Dogboy'. That's a first. Well, Dogboy here needs a punishment. He lost the race. I have another male over here who can't listen, he is in a world of his own. What do you say we punish both together?" Mistress Laura said laughing. "Well, I like that idea. Could be a lot of fun. What do you have in mind?" Mistress Janet said as she rested a sneaker clad foot on Dogboy's back.

Mistress Laura walked over to the blindfolded man and leaned down a little as she spoke to him "HELLO! Who is your Training Mistress? Can you hear me?" She spoke slowly and kind of loudly. The blindfolded man answered, "My training Mistress is Mistress Devon, Mistress." His voice strained from his position, but he did not move his nose from the grass. Mistress Laura raised her hand and looked over at the crowd. "Devon?" she shouted but no one came forward. "She isn't available at the moment." Mistress Janet answered. "She had an appointment." Mistress Laura walked over to me. She ran her fingers thru my hair. Then, without a word she turned and walked over to where Mistress Janet had her foot on 'Dogboy'. "What about 'Tractor'?" Mistress Laura asked. Mistress Janet took her foot off the man and stood up straight. "I love it! I was actually thinking the same thing. I'll get the stuff!" and she turned and walked toward the main building. "You should tell everyone, too." Mistress Laura said after her. "Okay! I will" Mistress Janet answered and skipped off. Mistress Laura took the tawse in her right hand and let a couple mild swats hit Dogboy's ass. He yelped. The crowd of women cheered and clapped. Then Mistress Laura turned her strap to the blindfolded man, and she did it quite a bit harder. He screamed in pain and agony as she kept hitting him. He had taken ten swats before she stopped and told him "When a woman is talking, any woman, you had better be listening. Is that clear to you?". The man was crying and moaning but he answered her "Yes Mistress". The crowd of women clapped their hands and laughed at his pain. I was really bothered by how much pleasure they were taking in watching this poor man be beaten. The mood amongst them reminded me of blood thirsty Romans at the colosseum hoping to see blood. They were charged up at his torment. They wanted more.

Mistress Janet returned holding a long rope. She handed one end to my Mistress and laid out the rope on the ground holding her end. She whistled and said "Come on. Here boy." And snapped her fingers. Dogboy turned and came to her. "Good boy!" she said patting his head. The rope had hooks on both ends of it. Mistress Laura attached the hook on her end of the rope to the end of the chastity cage on the blindfolded man. Mistress Janet attached the other to the chastity cage on Dogboy. They were about to make these men have a tug of war from their balls. Mistress Janet walked to the center of the rope and tied a ribbon. Mistress Laura slapped the blindfolded man on his ass and told him to "crawl forward!" and he did, taking up the slack in the rope. "When I say go, you two start pulling." More women had accumulated around this contest of the most disturbing nature. There was not going to be a winner. Both men are going to suffer. But that's the point, I thought to myself.

Mistress Janet took off her belt, folded it in half and held it by both ends making a loop. I was a woven fabric, not leather. But she handled it as if she knew how to use it. She was smiling ear to ear. So was my Mistress as she said "Ready. Set. Go!" The two men started crawling away from each other pulling on the rope by the chastity cages attached to their cocks and balls. Their faces told the story of how much pain they were in. Both Mistresses started whipping the asses of their charges. The belt seemed very effective in its implementation by Mistress Janet. Dogboy was pulling with everything he had and gained some ground right away. Mistress Laura brought the tawse down on the blindfolded man's ass in a fury, but it only resulted in his screams along with his half-hearted effort. His balls were bright red and when the tawse hit them as she leant down and cross strapped his lower cheeks and the top of his thighs, he really did start putting in the energy, dragging Dogboy back to where he had started from, but not much further. The crowd of women screamed in delight. They cheered, whistled and shouted rude comments. Both men continued being whipped, and it was clear from the way the chastity cages were stretched out that they were truly putting in the effort. It went on for what seemed like an hour, until my Mistresses' tawse again found the blindfolded man's scrotum. He screamed bloody murder and pulled so hard against the rope Dogboy couldn't even remain on his hands, falling on his face as he was pulled 15 feet past the start point. The contest was over. Both men were sobbing loudly as the ropes were unhooked from their cages. They were allowed to lay there on the ground for a few minutes after being inspected for any obvious damage. Mistress Laura helped the blindfolded man to his feet and removed the tear-soaked blindfold. "Assume your place over there at position 2." She told him softly while wiping his tears away. Mistress Janet was giving similar attention to Dogboy. The crowd of women were still laughing and talking as they walked back to the main building.

We drilled positions one thru four until the sun was getting low. Class was dismissed and Mistress Laura headed back to her apartment with me following her on my hands and my knees. I felt happy to be going home and I felt happy I had not fucked up today. My Mistress had not had to correct me at all. I felt pride. I certainly felt respect for her, and I was proud she was my training Mistress. Once inside the apartment, I was allowed to stand. As the night before she gave me a bath and dried me off. She used me to give her an orgasm with my tongue before she covered up and went to sleep. I laid down on my pallet and covered up. I enjoyed the taste and the odor of her sex on my face as I fell asleep, too, dreaming of how lucky I was and how glad I was that I took a chance on my dreams. I was right where I needed to be to get where I wanted to be.

Graduation Day

I could feel the gloved hand, and two fingers probing my anus. Pushing lube inside me with one finger, then with two. My cock was straining against the stainless-steel cage. My prisoner penis ached. I was blindfolded and I had no idea who it was that was finger fucking my ass. The room was full of women, and while it was quiet for the most part, I could hear them breathing. I could hear some whispers. Some giggles. Mistress Laura was allowing the owners to use me as part of her instruction for the women who had their men here at the academy. She was teaching them how to milk my prostrate. She had taught them how to drain all of the stored semen without giving me an orgasm, and why that was important for keeping a man full of desire and compliant to his Mistress. She showed them on the chalk board with illustrations and told them how to do it, but how the class started was with them learning how to, and then giving me a thorough enema. A more embarrassing day, I have never had.

The woman who had two fingers inside me now clumsily attempted to stroke my (as they were told) 'walnut sized' prostrate, but she wasn't doing a very good job. I wasn't sure about this anyway. I didn't believe my semen could be extracted without having some type of orgasm. I was bent over a table and tied down for this. My legs spread as far as they could go, bent at the knee and tied that way. The smell of perfume was thick in the room and my nose was itching. I knew better than to complain. I had never been penetrated by anyone who wasn't a doctor before. The feeling of her fingers in my ass wasn't exactly unpleasant, but not very intimate either. I felt like a specimen used for scientific research, and in fact, that is really what I was, I guess. An instructional tool. When she finally did find my prostrate, I let out a moan involuntarily. "Aha!" she exclaimed as she began squeezing and rubbing it. "Oh. Oh. Uh-Uh OH! OH! OH!" I moaned more as she moved her hand in and out.

"Okay! You found it. Let's give someone else a turn. Who's next?" Mistress Laura said. The woman removed her fingers and stepped away. I could hear another pair of gloves being put on, and the woman removing the gloves she had just pulled from me. "I never thought I would be doing this." A woman said and then giggled. "This is so exciting!" I felt a hand run over my ass cheeks. Then there was a loud 'smack!' as my ass was slapped. She pushed two lubed fingers into me with a single rough motion. I exclaimed "AHHH!" in pain. My sphincter tightened, clenching the fingers. She just started moving them in and out quickly and roughly. She stopped and squirted more lube onto my asshole and then continued pumping her hand back and forth. "Remember what I said, easy. Slow. You are not trying to fuck him. You are trying to milk him." My Mistress said. The woman stopped then instantly found my prostrate and stroked it with her fingers. The pain turned into pleasure. I started moaning again. It was quite pleasurable. I felt so full as she curled her fingers down and pulled me towards her. I could feel the warm semen as it worked itself out of my prisoner penis. She was rocking me back and forth causing my cock and balls to swing with the added weight of the cock cage, slinging my seminal fluid causing it to splash around, some of it hitting my thigh and running down my leg. Some of the women were laughing.

"That's it! You got it!" My Mistress said. "Pay attention everyone and watch how she is milking it out. And he isn't having an orgasm, nor is he ejaculating. His desire will remain high. He is programed by nature to ejaculate. Periodically draining his prostrate without ejaculation is the best way to keep him both healthy and compliant. You take control of nature when you can both keep his needy interest and satisfy his need to unload his juice. Have you ever experienced a man's disinterest in you after he ejaculates? He was all over you until you let him fuck you, right? Then as soon as HE comes, the attention stops! Even if you aren't done, he is. Well, here is the answer to that. He will still have the need to ejaculate, thus you keep his attention and the promise of you allowing him to ejaculate will keep him compliant. If you never milk him, or allow him to ejaculate, he will lose all interest in you and nature will cause him to wander, go find another way to ejaculate. Or…. He will become completely useless, and lose all motivation to please you." I could hear laughter and commotion as the woman stopped pumping me and removed herself from my ass. I could tell that it was my Mistress who stepped up behind me and put both of her hands on my ass cheeks. The way she touched me filled my heart with complete love for her. I longed for her touch.

"There is a more fun and less clinical way to milk him. A more empowering way to make him drain that poison and assert your authority at the same time." she said. She removed her right hand and pressed something into my well lubed anus. It felt giant and caused me to lose my breath as it slowly entered me. She stopped and held her position. "Strap on a dildo and fuck him. Make him know that he is the bitch in the relationship! Your bitch!" and with that she rammed the dildo all the way in me. I felt every muscle in my body tense up and then go weak. She pulled back slowly, and I could feel every inch of the dildo. I could feel the contour of the veins, the bulb of the head. I could feel how long it was. I could barely catch my breath as she slammed it all the way back inside me. Her nails dug into my skin where she held me with both hands on my hips. I was helpless to move, and she had her way with me, thrusting in and out to a rhythm she alone had in her head. The crowd of women were roaring with laughter and astonishment, and they cheered her on. Some of them shouted "I'm next!" or "My turn! My turn!" as my Mistress fucked me in front of them. The feeling was indescribable.

"You can do whatever you want in your house, Ladies. But in MY house, I do the fucking. My slave will always know who is in charge. Even if I felt the need to have his cock and if I let him fuck me, I remain in charge. This is the norm he can expect. Serving me, suffering for me, getting fucked by me. I harness the powerful natural drive he creates for himself in his testicles, and I use it against him. For his benefit of course, a male needs a woman in charge." My mistress said to them. While she talked, she slowed herself down, but kept fucking me. I was shooting cum all over the place. I wasn't having an orgasm in the way I was accustomed, but it was like I was having a continuing orgasm. I was seeing stars and the world was spinning. I could not have understood before that moment. It was a new pleasure. I was in love with my Mistress. I felt warm all over and I felt full. Full but not violated as I had before. I felt her every move and the way she grabbed at my haunches. I was alive with sensation. I could feel her fingerprints on my skin. The way the dildo she was fucking me with felt was like she was stroking my cock inside my body, only it wasn't my cock. This felt ten times better than the best blow job I had ever had. I was in pure ecstasy. She pumped me hard again and again, I literally squealed like a girl from the pleasure. I felt completely submissive to her. Suddenly she removed her dildo from me. I felt empty. Lost. Exhausted. I was completely wasted. All my muscles weak from use. She left me there like that. I could hear her removing her harness, the Velcro ripping, and then she laid the dildo still attached to the harness on the small of my back. I started crying for some reason. The release I felt mixed with so many emotions. I was told all my life that this was a bad thing. That it was what a sissy might do. A reprehensible act. All of that is wrong. I wasn't gay, and I knew that. Funny thought about how good it made me feel, how happy, and gay means happy. Who could possibly think bad about a person for being happy?

"Look at him ladies. A well-disciplined, and a well-fucked male. He will follow any command. Follow every rule you have. He will be of service to you. In any capacity you require. It won't make them smarter, although it will seem like it since you will make decisions for them. It won't make them better looking, but they will be healthier following the diet and exercise you choose for them. It won't make them rich, but they will perform at a higher level at work as well as home. It will make them obedient and loyal. Compliant to YOUR wishes. All of them." Mistress Laura walked over and stroked my hair, and I felt joy at her touch. I was in love with her. She continued talking to the women: "Well that's it. This is the final class. I have some instructional manuals for care of your males, read it this week. Tips on how to do everything from how to speak to him, to how to spank him. There is an illustration of positions for him and hand signals you can use, a guide for how to buy a strap-on dildo and how to use it correctly. How to clean your male, and your strap-on, before and after use. Milking instruction, edging tips, ruined orgasm tips."

My mistress reached down and wiped my tears away. She then untied me and grabbed me by the hair and pulled me up until I was standing. My cock strained against its cage, a prisoner. But it felt so good, everything felt good right now.

"Graduation day is tomorrow. Be here by noon to inspect your male. If you don't accept him, and you are not obligated to, there are options ranging from further training, to open auction where he will be sold, and a portion of the proceeds will go to you. Our trained slaves frequently sell for quite a lot. But after they are sold, you will not see them again. It is a rather final decision. 12 will be auctioned to some very lucky buyer. He is what we call a 'surrender', he applied himself to our program, and he has done very well from the start." Her hand lifted my caged cock, cupping my balls to lift it gently. "His balls empty, but still full of the natural desire to ejaculate, which he did not do, he will do my biding without question. And that is the goal, ladies. That is why we are here." She let go of my balls letting them fall freely. She was right. I would have done anything she asked. She made me Her's. Her property. Her slave. Her devoted anything she wanted.

I had been at the academy for nine months. Day after day of abuse, training, exercise, and horrible meals. Treated and fed like a dog. Hours and hours of learning how to sit. How to stand. How to cook. How to make tea. The proper way to clean. I had been used as furniture. I had not worn any clothes besides an apron when cooking. I was lovingly cared for. Bathed each night before bedtime, where I was allowed to worship at her alter. Before today the only sexual pleasure I had been allowed was pleasing her. Today I was fucked. Publicly. And I loved every second of my Mistress fucking me. Through it all Mistress Laura had been both cruel and loving. And, this is exactly what I have needed all of my life. I have needed order and discipline. Punishment and correction. Total domination.

She put me on my hands and knees and said goodbye to the ladies. Some of them gave her a hug. All of them seemed extremely happy. One woman reached down and grabbed my balls and squeezed them on her way out the door. The remaining women all started laughing. Then another woman slapped my ass with her hand.

I was led back to Mistress Laura's apartment and again bathed. It was different because the sun was still up. Mistress Laura usually did not bath me until later in the evening unless I was filthy from training. I was frequently filthy from training, but on those occasions, I typically was not back at my Mistress's apartment to be bathed until after sundown. "You did good today, 12. I am proud of you." She said to me as she soaped my skin with the sponge. "Thank you, Mistress" I responded. The odor of the bath salts filled the air. Lavender, I think. I loved it. "Turn over." She told me and I did exactly as she asked. she reached between my legs and lifted me by my chastity cage until my ass was up. She then started soaping my ass. It did feel nice having her attention. My erection, of course, was restrained as usual, but that did not stop the effort of my cock getting hard. When she was done, she pulled the drain plug and left me there in the tub, on my knees. As the water drained, she began undressing. Her naked body was a truly marvelous thing to see. I felt so lucky. She opened the glass door to the shower stall and turned on the water. "Come here and join me in the shower." I was on my feet quickly. She removed the chain that held a key on it from around her neck and unlocked the lock on my chastity cage. She then removed the locking pin and removed the chastity cage. My cock sprang up. There were imprints on the head of my cock from wearing the chastity cage for so long. She set the cage on the counter with the lock and key then grabbed my cock firmly, squeezing it hard. It was all I could do to keep my hands at my side. I wanted to grab her breast, touch her body. Nine months. It had been nine months since anyone, including myself, had touched my cock. I was overwhelmed with emotions.

She opened the door to the shower stall again and led me inside by my cock. The shower stall was a standard size, and it had a bench opposite the shower head. Our bodies were against each other, and she let go of my cock, which pointed straight out and against her thigh. She ran both hands up my chest and grabbed my head, pulling me to her lips. She kissed me deeply for the first time. She had kissed me before, but closed lips and little pecks on the forehead or cheek. Not like this. Not romantic like this. I kissed her back, and it was the most passionate kiss of my life. It lasted at least five minutes. My mind was completely clear of anything but her. Her lips were full and soft. Her breath was hot and sweet. Her tongue was wrestling mine. Her hands were holding my head, pulling my hair hard. I didn't feel any pain at all, or, at least I didn't mind it. She seemed to really like pulling my hair, as she did it often. My hands were on her shoulders, and I caressed her back, stopping at the small of her back above her beautiful bottom.

She broke off the kiss. "You are a great kisser, 12. That was amazing. Now sit down on this bench." I did as she instructed, and she handed me a bar of soap and a washcloth from the shelf in the corner of the stall. I began soaping and washing her body. She had not let me do this before, and I wish she had. The feel of her soaped-up skin was heavenly. Washing her breast, lifting them to wash under them. The weight of her breast, so soft and round, aroused me even more. Her body was perfect. There truly must be a God to have created such wonderful creatures as women. I loved everything about her. Even her cruel treatment of me while punishing me. I loved her. I was proud to suffer for her. Having cleaned everything above her knee she raised her legs one at a time, setting her foot on top of my cock resting on the bench, and allowed me to wash between her legs, her beautiful vagina, and down to her calf and her beautiful feet. Once I had done that, she told me to stand on the bench and shampoo her hair. As I poured a small amount of shampoo in my hand and started caressing it into her hair, she started stroking my cock, cupping my balls in her left hand. Her head was parallel to my groin. She tilted her head to keep the shampoo out of her eyes. I used the handheld shower head to rinse her hair. Running my fingers through her hair to aid in the rinsing. I washed it twice and conditioned it, taking my time. After I was done, I rinsed her body off using the handheld shower head then switched the shower to the stationary head. The water was at the perfect temperature and pointed straight at her bottom. Her hand was still stroking me. She had stopped while

I was rinsing her and just held on like my cock was a handle. Suddenly she let go and stared at my cock. I had lowered my hands to my side, not knowing what I should do with them. She looked up at me, smiled, and said "Stay.". then she turned, turned off the water, and left the shower. She grabbed a towel and dried herself off. She wrapped the towel around her waist and used another towel to dry her hair, wrapping it turban style on her head. With her beautiful breast exposed, she left the room without even looking my direction.

Having spent one hundred percent of the last nine months nude, I had long ago become accustomed to being cold. Every night sleeping on the floor next to my Mistress' bed I had struggled with being cold. Believe me when I tell you that standing there on the bench in the shower, wet, I was the coldest I had ever been in my life, before or since. My arousal was gone, and now my totally free penis shrank to a shadow of what it once was. I had never seen it so small. I suppose nine months caged influenced it. I was crying and shivering when she returned.

"Oh, just climb down, you big baby!" she shouted at me. "Come out here!" she was holding four fingers pointed down and I wasted zero time getting out of the shower and on my hands and knees at her feet.

She was no longer wearing the towels. She wasn't wearing anything at all. She was however holding a riding crop in her hand. Being at her feet on my hands and my knees the blood began to flow back into penis. I started to warm up all over again. She ran the leather blade of the riding crop down the center of my back to my ass as she walked around behind me. She tapped me on my ass cheeks with it a couple times. She straddled me and sat down on my hips. I could feel the heat from her beautiful vagina against my skin. Her weight on my hips was no problem for me at all. Her legs were bent at the knee and her toes were on the floor, she didn't have any weight on her feet.

She grabbed a fistful of my hair in one hand, pulled my head back. I felt the riding crop strike on my right ass cheek as she said: "Giddy up!" I started moving, slowly towards the restroom door. She kept her balance using her feet. Then as we reached the glorious, padded carpet of her bedroom, she landed another skillful smack against my ass with the riding crop as she pulled my head left by my hair, apparently indicating I should turn left. I did just that and she rode me like a horse into the living room. She kept expertly using the riding crop striking me in the same exact spot as we entered the living room and made a circle around the couch a couple of times. She turned me by pulling my hair in the direction she wished to go. I could hear her giggle over my breathing which had become rather loud and actually horse like.

Finally, she pulled back on my hair and told me: "Whoa boy!" when we were directly in front of the coffee table. I stopped and she stood up, our skin was sticking together in some areas and the separation caused both of us to wince a little. She reached down and caressed the ass cheek that she had been cropping. Lovingly. Soothingly. Then walked in front of the coffee table and held four fingers down over it. I climbed up on the table. Her nudeness in front of me was so intoxicating. She grabbed my hair as she raised her exquisite left leg over my shoulder and pulled my mouth to her divine wet center. I tried to lap at her, I could barely make contact using my tongue. She rubbed her clit on my nose before removing herself from me and leaving me there for what felt like an hour. I loved the way she smelled, and I savored her exquisite essence.

The table was not huge. I just had enough room put my hands and my knees on the corners of it. As coffee tables go it was overbuilt for its size. Large sturdy post on the corners making it very stable. The top was made of two by six boards pinned together and framed with the same material vertically skirting the top and adjoined at the corners in forty-five-degree angles. It was stained dark mahogany. The four posts were turned on a lathe and had two rounded areas on them that looked like balls banded together. I had not noticed before then that there were eye bolts on the underside of the tabletop skirting. My knees were starting to ache from the use, and I had returned to being cold once again. My manhood, although freed from its prison, dangled quite limp and shriveled between my legs as I labored to remain in the position that my Mistress left me in.

My mind drifted and I remembered a girl I had dated right after high school. She was still in school at the time. When we went out alone, we would drive to an old, abandoned rock quarry and we would make out. She liked to straddle me while I sat in the passenger seat, and she would ride me. I thought at the time that we were in love and that we would get married someday. But it turned out that I was only a dick for her to ride until a bigger dick came along. She made me feel very worthless, and my heart was broken. I didn't feel worthless anymore. Not now that I had found my purpose in life. There on the table on my hands and knees, cold and naked, suffering for my Mistress, I didn't feel worthless at all. I felt proud. Proud to give her all I had. Proud to be hers. I remember smiling as I heard her behind me say: "I have a surprise for you, 12."

I really couldn't imagine what the surprise might be. Today was already full of so many surprises. I had been used as a training tool that had strange women putting their fingers in my ass. My

Mistress had fucked me with a dildo in front of that group of women. I had been allowed to join her in the shower and clean her body. I had been ridden like a horse around the apartment. What else could be about to happen? "Stand up." She said softly. I rose to my feet, slowly. It felt so good to stand up, I couldn't help from stretching. I stood there stretching out all over. I guess I had been stretching too long because my Mistress walked up to me and grabbed me by my balls and squeezed. Hard. I went blind with a white flash of pain in my eyes causing every muscle in my body to tense up at once, doubling me over at the waist.

"I said stand up! Not dance like a noodle! What the hell is your problem suddenly?" she used a very low and angry tone as she squeezed. When she let go of my balls, the ache I felt in my eyes slowly left. Then she softly began stroking my cock. Her soft touch and slow movement got me hard very quickly. She had me close to the point of no return in about three heart beats, and then she let go of my cock again. Somehow, she produced the riding crop again and she smacked my throbbing erection with it. It hurt, but it also felt amazing. I was still throbbing and so desperate for her touch, that even the pain she delivered felt amazing. We stood there for a moment, facing each other, not making eye contact. Her eyes were watching my frustrated erection bob up and down. I was looking straight up at the ceiling as I had been trained to do.

"I would like a glass of wine." She said to me. "Bring it to me in the bedroom." Then she turned and walked into the bedroom again. I loved watching her walk, the way her beautiful legs lifted her beautiful ass cheeks with each step. I pivoted and sprang into action, my still hard cock pointing the way to the wine bottle in the refrigerator door. I poured her a glass of her Pinot and made my way for her bedroom. My rigged cock still arriving just before me. She was standing next to the bed, and I knelt in front of her and offered her up the glass of wine, my head down, as I had been trained.

She took the glass as she put her hand in my hair with her other hand. She drank from the glass, I could hear her lick her lips as she set the glass down on the table. She moved towards the edge of the bed and sat down and pulled me to her and pushed my head between her legs. She laid back and raised her legs giving me full access to her divine sex. I ran my tongue from the bottom to the top of the sweet moist folds of her exquisite pussy, and back down again a few times before I thrust my tongue into her opening just once, then after I lapped at her some more, I pushed my tongue into her again and held it there. She moaned in pleasure as I endeavored to push my tongue as deep into her as I could. I sucked hard on her engorged clitoris, and she threw her hands over her head as she screamed when she reached her first orgasm. Then she quickly pushed my head away from her and she caught her breath. I knew that she got very sensitive after she climaxed, and I wasn't surprised that she pushed my head away. She did that almost every night. My cock was hard. I wanted to fuck her so badly.

Then, as if she was reading my mind, she said "fuck me, 12. Fuck me right now! I want your cock inside me!" and I needed no more encouragement than that as I rose to my feet and without even using my hands to guide it, my cock head pressed against her heavenly opening. Her eyes closed as I pressed into her, the feeling of her extremely hot and slippery wet vagina squeezing very hard against my long-deprived cock had me ready to cum instantly. "You do not have permission to cum until I tell you to!" she shouted at me. And then the urge to cum had passed. I picked up the pace and began thrusting harder and harder until I was literally pounding her. She screamed as she orgasmed, and she squeezed my cock hard when she did. I could not control it when I exploded inside of her. I didn't slow my pace and she came again. Her eyes were wide open, and her mouth was open as she both grunted and breathed thru her mouth. I saw her eyes turn to anger and I knew I was in for it. I did keep thrusting into her a few more times, but I saw her arousal disappear and she suddenly pushed me away. In a single motion she was on her feet and punching me in my stomach. She ran into the bathroom, and I was left standing bent over from the sudden pain she dealt me with her punch.

I was on all fours as she dealt the first blow. She was using something I had not had experience with yet. It was truly excruciating. It felt like a knife cutting into me. Mistress Laura was wailing on my ass using little if any restraint. She was genuinely angry, and she was quiet as she displayed her displeasure onto me. Whenever she had beat me in the past, she had been quite vocal about the lesson I was to be learning. Understanding that the trust I had betrayed had hurt her, and that she had been so sweet to me before I fucked it up, I did not protest her brutal assault on me. I knew that I deserved everything she gave me, if not more. I was angry with myself and wanted to suffer. I wanted her punishment. I needed it. I knew I fucked up seriously and that I destroyed her trust in me. I wish that I could explain why it happened, what caused my lack of control after dreaming every night of how making love to her would feel. How it would go. Having my opportunity to show her my devotion. Then I get my chance, my only chance in nine months and I fuck it up so bad she would not even scream at me. When she came out of the restroom, she only said "On your knees, asshole." with nearly no emotion.

Mistress Laura was a very passionate woman of power. She commanded respect not only from me and from the other males here, but also from her female peers. She was a woman to be respected. Obeyed. When given the very personal invitation to penetrate her, I did so like a teenaged moron with no self-discipline, and thereby destroying her trust in me. I hurt her. As she delivered perhaps the fiftieth blow to my ass, a very strange thing had happened. The pain turned into pleasure somehow. I went from crying from the pain to feeling very aroused. My penis, still not locked, and also still damp from her heavenly exquisite juices, began to come alive. I felt orgasmic again as she continued to swipe the devilish object into my flesh. As she slowed down, I supposed from physical exhaustion, my cock became harder and harder, and I neared an orgasm again. I was confused and my eyes stung from crying, her beating was real, and it hurt, but now I was feeling pleasure from the blows. Orgasmic pleasure. When she noticed the erection, and my response of leaning into her blows instead of away from them, she stopped altogether hitting me. I think that it surprised her too.

"Stand up!" she shouted at me. "On your feet, and I mean now!!" I stood as fast as I could, facing her I put my hands behind my back and my head down, as I had been trained to do. "Stroke yourself." She said. Her tone was now one of amusement. My cock was once again hard and I began stroking myself with my right hand, leaving my left one behind my back. I stroked my cock fully from the base to the tip and then back again, slowly. "Faster!" she said loudly in her amused voice. Increasing the pace, I noticed that her juices on my cock had dried and now were sticky. I thought to myself that I could use some spit for lubrication, but I didn't dare speak. Or stop. Or even slow down. I just continued as she watched. She began rubbing her glorious clit. While she did, she put her other hand on the top of my head, which was still looking down, and grabbed a fistful of hair into her fist. She didn't pull, she just held my head as I was working my hand on my shaft.

"I want you to tell me when you are about to cum, 12." She said softly to me. I wanted to kiss her so badly. She was still rubbing her clit left and right, keeping time with my strokes, holding a fist full of my hair in her other hand. This woman was so damned sexy. I literally worshipped her. I was in love, and it felt so amazing. When she used that tone of voice on me, I felt like I my heart was melting, I know it sounds cheesy, but it is exactly how it felt. Her exquisite power over me was so complete. She had been cruel. Her abuse of me was intense at times, and I didn't enjoy much of it at all. Even if it was coming to an end, I felt so lucky to be with her.

I was nearing an orgasm and she must have sensed it because she commanded me to stop in that same sweet soft voice. I dropped my hand and returned it behind my back to be with my other hand. My cock bobbed and the rush of desperation to be touched filled my body. She continued rubbing her clit as I watched her. She picked up the pace and she started breathing heavily before she tensed up and stopped moving her hand. She was pulling my hair hard for a second, and she let out a loud moan of pleasure that seemed to go on for minutes. Then she relaxed and she rubbed her very wet pussy. She moved her fingers up and down into the folds of her exquisite labia as I watched. My cock was still very hard, but my urgent need to cum had passed. She brought her sopping wet fingers up to my mouth. I instinctually opened my mouth as she pushed them in. Without being told I sucked them as she moved her hand around to make sure I could get all of her sweet nectar. The taste of her was amazing and I cleaned her hand as she pulled my hair with the other one. My erection was still between us.

She removed her fingers from my mouth, and I sighed a little bit. That made her giggle. "You and I need to eat something. Clean yourself and make us both a sandwich." She said in that sweet voice of hers that made me want to put my arms around her and kiss her deeply. She let go of my hair and softly rubbed my ass cheeks, which felt amazing.

My erection subsided until I put on my apron. The feel of the material against my still free penis aroused me and I became hard again. I was nearly finished making sandwiches when Mistress Laura came into the kitchen. She was still nude, her now dried hair in a ponytail. She walked up behind me and reached between my legs from behind and grabbed my balls, giving them a gentle squeeze. Her hand felt amazing. She stroked my hair with her other hand and pushed her body against mine causing me to put my hands on the counter to hold myself. The sandwiches were both ready, all I had left to do was to cut them in half. "Turn around" she said firmly. As I did, she pulled my apron to the side, knelt down and took my cock into her mouth. She took in most of me at once, withdrew and then took my entire length until her nose was pressed up against me. She held there, feeling me throb in her mouth for a heartbeat or two then withdrew again completely. She caught her breath and licked the tip of my cock before she took in just the head and sucked. She sucked the head of my cock hard. I was leaning back, pressed against the kitchen counter, the sandwiches on the cutting board behind me. I had my hands holding the edge of the counter, my back arched. I was watching this beautiful woman with my cock in her mouth when she looked up at me, and her eyes smiled. I swear to God, she smiled with her eyes. Then she closed her eyes and started moving her head up and down, taking me into her mouth. I was so close to cumming, trying to resist. "I am about to cum!" I said, panting. But she didn't stop. "I am going to cum!" I said more urgently this time, but she kept on slowly moving her mouth up and down on me. I couldn't hold back much longer when she reached back up and grabbed my testicles in one hand and squeezed. I exploded and she buried my cock deep inside her throat. I ejaculated down her throat as her hand squeezed my balls harder and harder. She held me there for a moment before pulling back up. She caught her breath and released the squeeze she had on my balls, but did not let go. Then she went back down part way and squeezed my balls again. My whole body was shaking from pleasure. As she sucked my cock and squeezed my balls, I could feel every last drop of the semen I had in my body travel the length of my still hard, but softening penis. When she was satisfied that I had nothing left, and my cock was obviously soft in her mouth, she removed me from her mouth. She squeezed my balls one last time for good measure, watching to see if more cum escaped, then let go of my balls and stood up. She looked me in the eye and smiled as she wiped the mixture of saliva and cum from her mouth with her hand. She offered her hand to my mouth to clean for her, and I did. Greedily. She smiled at that. "Get on your knees, 12." She said musically. As I got down, she ran her fingers lovingly thru my hair. I looked up at her, and she smiled at me.

"I told you I had a surprise for you. Were you surprised?" she asked me. "Yes Mistress." I truthfully answered her. The endorphins were swimming around in my brain, and my whole body felt like jelly. She turned towards the counter and without a word picked up the knife and sliced both sandwiches in half. She picked up one half and took a bite. She set the sandwich down and cut the other sandwich into smaller bite sized pieces. She set down the knife and picked up the half she had already started and took another bite while she picked up one of the smaller pieces and fed it to me while I knelt in front of her. "You can touch me." She told me in between bites. Having her permission, I put both hands on her hips and caressed her buttocks and thighs while she fed me my sandwich, one bite at a time.

"This is our last night together, 12. I wanted to make it a special night for both of us. You have been a very, very good student. You sure will make a wonderful slave to some lucky woman, 12. Tomorrow you graduate the academy, and you will be sold." My eyes began to tear up as she talked to me. The thought of being sent away from her, from there, made me very sad. I was feeling emotions I had not expected. "Don't cry, 12. You will be fine. I understand it might be hard, but I am your training Mistress, and you are trained. Time for you to enter service to your new owner. Tonight, you may sleep in my bed with me, if you like. Would you like that, 12?" she was looking down smiling at me and still playing with my hair. "Oh yes, Mistress! I would like that very much!

I woke up with my head on her stomach, and her hand on my arm. She had held me all night. I had cried myself to sleep. She was sweet, understanding and patient with me. She consoled me, and I had felt loved. I didn't want it to end. She was already awake, and she had let me sleep. But now that I was awake, she wanted to get up. She told me we had a big day and I needed to help her get ready. She had me make us coffee and toast to start while she had her shower and dressed. I was to shower after her while she had her coffee. She was going to style my hair for me. She entered the bathroom while I was in the shower and handed me a razor. "Shave yourself completely, carefully. I don't want any cuts on you when I put your cage back on you." She said seriously, looking me in the eye. "Is that understood?".

"Yes Mistress, I will be careful." I responded immediately. She stood back and watched me as I cleaned and shaved all of my pubic hair. I was careful to not cut myself, and it paid off. When I exited the shower, she was right there handing me a towel. "Dry off very good between your legs." She told me, and continued to watch me. She removed a hair dryer from a drawer and made sure my cock and balls were dry. She turned the hair dryer onto the cock cage that she apparently boiled and let cool, then she knelt down and put it on me. First the locking ring over my balls, then pulling my cock thru the ring. I started getting hard at her touch. She was ready for that and put an ice pack on my cock and held it there until my pesky erection subsided. She slipped the warm stainless-steel tube over my cock, inserted the locking pin, twisting the pin so that the threaded part of the pin was holding it all together tightly, then she reached over and grabbed the padlock and locked my cock away. I remember thinking that she would never unlock me again, that next time I was released it would be someone else that held my key. My new owner. I felt scared suddenly. Who knew what kind of a woman would buy me? I started to cry again. She slapped my ass. "Quit that right now! You have nothing to feel sad about!" I tried to keep my composure, and she started putting some gel into my hair. As she combed my hair she said "You are a good-looking man. I am sure you will fetch a high price at today's auction. The higher the price, the higher quality of your new owner. It is imperative that you make the best impression you can make. Two weeks from now I will have a new student, you will be with your new owner. This will be a wonderful memory for you, and for me. But you must smile and keep your eyes dry." She put the chain that held the key to my cock cage around her neck.

Being finished with me for the moment, she changed clothes again. She wore a white evening gown that was perfectly cut to hug and accentuate every curve of her body. It was low cut in the front, and it had an open back. It ever so slightly touched the floor until she had me put her shoes on her which were open toe high heel the same color as her gown, but the spike heel was chrome steel.

She attached my leash to my chastity cage lock, instructed me to get on my hands and my knees by using a hand signal. Then we were out the door and down the hall. When we had made it to the foyer and were making our way out the door, I looked back behind me to see for the last time a place that had changed my life forever. Remembering what Mistress Laura had said, I was determined to keep my shit together. I owed it to her. I owed it to myself.

When we arrived at the big house and I was making my way up the steps on my hands and my knees I remembered the first time I had done it, the day I surrendered and the day I met my Mistress. I remembered how afraid I was, and I realized how far I had come. I was completely amazed. I had no money, no home, no friends, no wife, no children. I had none of the things people used to measure success in life, but I felt as if I was a success. I had excelled in my training and had made myself of value. I had developed skills that I previously had not had. Well today, strangers, complete strangers, are going to assign a value to this. A quantitative value. A dollar amount of my worth. I suggest that few men in this day in age are ever afforded any such validation. Sure, they can say how much they are paid for their work. Or how much they have in the bank. But how much would a woman pay to own them? It had been my previous viewpoint that women looked to a man's worth as how much money he had, and what type of security he could offer them. This was truly an enlightened sect of women here. I had never heard of this type of woman before. The type of woman who demands quality men. Quality from men. Demands it. The funny thing is, most of it is just good old-fashioned manners. Manners and discipline.

We had entered the foyer of the big house and I saw that the hallway was lined up on both sides with men standing facing the wall. I was led down the hall between the rows of men to the end where Mistress Laura pointed to a spot with one finger, which meant I was to stand at that spot. I stood there facing the wall. I noticed a piece of paper on the wall above my head that said "12" on it.

I could hear women laughing and talking inside the lunchroom. I could smell them. The perfumes they wore all mixed together to make some type of flower garden odor. I could hear Mistress Raven start speaking, and the room get quiet as she did. But although I could hear her speaking, I was unable to make out what she was saying. Her voice seemed to rise and fall in volume. I could hear some of the men in the hallway with me breathing. I was thinking about the last nine months here when I heard Mistress Raven speak clearly in the hallway.

"Backs to the wall, Slaves. Heads down, eyes closed. You are to be examined. You may be questioned, answer the questions. You will cooperate with your examiner. Unless you are instructed to, remain with your eyes closed and your heads down." Mistress Raven always had a calm voice, and a commanding tone when she spoke. Her voice was replaced that of Mistress Brooke, who always sounded like she was having the best day of her life. "Okay ladies, they are ready for you out here in the hallway, you take your time, and if you have any questions for the training Mistresses, we will be right inside the lounge at the end of the hallway. Just remember the slave's number you have a question about." And I could hear her heels as she walked down the hallway to the lounge.

The women began filling up the hallway, high heel shoes banging against the hardwood floor. I could hear some of them asking questions of the other men. I started to wonder what was wrong with me because no one so much as even looked at me as far as I could tell. Then I remembered that these men had been brought here by their wives or their girlfriends or whatever. I could hear the lines of questioning that suggested familiarity. Some laughter. Some ridicule. Someone pinched my right nipple, and another person stuck a finger in my mouth, so I sucked on it, instinctually, you understand. When suddenly a woman asked me if I were bisexual. "No, Ma'am. I am not bisexual." I answered flatly without opening my eyes. I felt like it was an odd question to be asked, and there were no follow up questions. By the end of it I felt horrible. Then my Mistress, Mistress Laura was in front of me. I could smell her, sense her, I knew it was her before she spoke. "Your moment has not yet arrived, 12. You were a surrender. But you have been inquired about, and I need you to come with me." She put a blindfold over my eyes that plunged me into darkness. She reached down and grabbed the leash dangling from my cage and said: "On your knees, 12." I did as she asked, and she led me down the hall to a private room. "This is 12. He will submit to your examination and questions. Take as much time as you like with him." And she closed the door behind her as she left me on my hands and knees. She had left the handle of the leash draped around my neck.

"Please make yourself comfortable, 12." Said a woman who had a hauntingly familiar voice. I could not remember where, but I had heard that voice before. I brought myself to a relaxed position sitting back on my heels, with my knees apart. Just as I had been instructed. My hands were palm up, resting on my thighs. The "wait' position. "12, Do you like what you are doing?" asked the woman. "Yes Ma'am." I answered quickly. A few moments passed before she asked me "How do you feel being auctioned off to a total stranger? To be owned by someone. Someone you have never met. With no say in the matter. You don't know what you are going to get, do you?" I considered her question, but really, not for long. I had been asking myself the very same questions for a long time now. I answered truthfully.

"Ma'am, it seems to me that nobody knows what they will have, ultimately. I know from experience that nothing is guaranteed in life. I feel that being auctioned; I will at least be with someone who wants me. Someone who is invested in me. That improves my chances of being cared for properly. I desire to be of service, and to please women. I have endeavored to be the best I can be, to that end. A stranger is only a person I have not yet met. I feel a little bit scared, though." I felt like I was starting to ramble.

"That's fine, 12, but what about not having a say in the matter? How does that make you feel, and why are you okay with that?" She asked again. I had messed up. I had not answered her question completely making her have to ask me again. I was so distracted trying to place her voice. I know I have heard it before. I needed to focus. "I apologize, Ma'am. Before I surrendered myself to this program, I had come to realize that I was a submissive man. I believe in female supremacy, and I knew that I liked women making my decisions for me. I surrendered to this program completely. To this lifestyle. I walked away from any notion that I am qualified to run my life, which had never been of any use to anyone. Including myself." I could hear the words I was saying, and I wondered to myself if I sounded crazy. "How about if you were to be given away by your owner to a new owner?" She asked me. I had thought about that before. "I have no problem with that, Ma'am."

"Ok. Now, about sex. How would you describe your, limitations? Is there a hard limit you have? Something that you will refuse to do? Even if instructed to by your owner?" She asked me in an assured tone. "Ma'am, I will be at service to my owner. Whatever is required of me I will endeavor to perform at the highest level I can." I thought that was understood, but I guess not. "What if your owner only wants you as entertainment for guest, or loans you out to friends for services?" I gave her the exact same answer with no attitude whatsoever: "Ma'am, I will be at service to my owner. Whatever is required of me I will endeavor to perform at the highest level I am able."

"Okay, 12. There are no more questions. I would like you to stand and turn slowly around a couple of times for me." I did as she instructed. "Ok, 12. I have what I need. You may leave now." I felt around for the door and found the doorknob. Exiting the door and closing it behind me, I stood facing the wall in the hallway until my Mistress found me only moments later. She took hold of my leash, and I went down on my hands and knees without being told too and she took me back up the hallway, her chromed steel spike heels making a distinctive sound on the hardwood floor. I noticed, even though I was blindfolded, that the other men were not in the hall any longer. I was led into the lunchroom and told to "wait". I rose and rested on my heels, knees spread and palms up on my thighs. I could hear some women talking, but not as many as before. After a while I heard Mistress Raven say: "Let's get the lights ready."   There was some commotion and I heard Mistress Raven saying something low that I could not understand. Then she started talking louder. "Okay! Okay! Alright!" she was clapping her hands, everyone in the room started clapping their hands also. "We have had another successful graduating class with 100% acceptance! This is huge. Let us give the training Mistresses a big round of applause, they are truly doing a wonderful job!!" The women were all clapping. "Now we have only one left for your consideration. He is what we call a 'surrender'. He paid for and applied himself to this program for his own reasons. You will find him a truly rare specimen, as I do. With that said, let's hear from his training Mistress, Mistress Laura!" There was a big round of applause, and I could hear her walking across the room. "Thank you, Thank you all. And I would like to thank you, Mistress Raven. Thank you for keeping this dream that the founder, Mistress Jessica Yang, had all those decades ago. She was a woman who was truly ahead of her time. Can we all give some applause for her? Can we? WOW!" the room erupted in applause and women were yelling. It seemed all of them were standing. "WOW! Yes. Yes! Yes!! Without her guiding principles and forward thinking, where in the world would we be today?" The roar of applause continued. "Okay. Okay. I am up here to talk to you about 12. He is up for auction today. I have been his training Mistress, but I cannot take all of the credit for his results. The whole staff of training Mistresses here took part in his training. He has been in my charge since he arrived. I have spent every night and most all everyday with him. He has been my favorite trainee. He has applied himself to his training. As we all know, men are never completely trained. How simple would life be if we could tell them to do something once and they would continue the behavior. Show them how you like something, and for them to do it right from then on. How great would that be? How great would it be if they never forgot their manners and never embarrassed us? If I could change anything about men, I would make them WOMEN!" The room erupted in applause. My Mistress had them all in the palm of her hand. "I have trained over 20 men here. 12 is the only one who has got it completely. He is ready to offer a life of servitude with the least adjustment that you could find in any man. For the size of the investment, you would be making, that is what you expect. We stand behind our training. We stand behind our recommendations. I personally guarantee satisfaction with this slave. Okay if we could lower the lights, please Mistress Brooke, Thank you. Ladies we took some of your questions and we condensed them into a few, and we had a professional interviewer come in, someone you are sure to recognize, she asks these questions directly to 12 for us. We videotaped the whole thing." And with that I heard the video start. I heard the woman who talked to me, and I knew then where I had heard her voice. She was one of those morning show host, one of those on the networks, I could not remember which, Katie something. Or Kathy. Hell, I could not remember.

They played the interview and there were some whispers from the women. When it was almost over my Mistress walked up to me and grabbed my leash. I followed her over to the stage that was set up and I climbed on to it. When the video was done playing, Mistress Laura told me to stand up. As I rose, she removed my Blindfold. Thankfully, the lights were dim, but my eyes still needed to adjust. After only a few moments though, there was a spotlight pointed at me. I could not see anyone in the audience. I could see Mistress Laura, who was holding my leash and standing back at the podium. "Here he is. We feel confident you will agree, we are going to start his bid off at ten thousand dollars. This will be a silent auction, and you can use your smartphones to bid. You all have been given this information, but just to be clear about the rules before the bidding starts. 1. All bids are confidential. 2. All bids are a commitment as agreed to in the contract. 3. The highest bid in the time limit of 15-minutes from the opening of the bid will be the declared winner, and any bids after the 15-minute time limit will be void. 4. Funding is required immediately following the close of the auction. Winner of the bid is to take possession immediately following the auction, but arrangements could be made if needed. We have bidders online who will be bidding as well."

My Mistress turned to me. I was shaking I was so nervous. My eyes had adjusted, and I could now see that there were about 20 women in the room. They were all quiet and looking at their phones. Mistress Raven was on the stage, and she walked center to the stage and announced: "Ladies, the bidding has started. Please place your online bids at this time."

The time went slow. My Mistress stood beside me and ran her

hand lovingly over my back and my shoulders. She patted my butt a couple of times. She turned to me and whispered: "You are doing great. Good job, 12. I am so proud of you." I replied to her "Thank you, Mistress." Then Mistress Raven announced: "Ladies, the bidding has concluded, and we have a winning bid. I would like to thank all of you for your interest, we look forward to seeing you at future auctions. Today's event is over, however, please see yourselves out at your leisure, there are still plenty of refreshments and snacks. Thank you again." The lights came on and the spotlight went out. Mistress Laura directed me to follow her, and I went down on all fours again, following her out into the hall. She gave my leash a firm tug, I think just being playful. Still being attached to my cock cage it smarted a little, but it made me smile all the same. She led me to the stairwell and up to the second floor and into the offices. I was told to "Wait" outside the door to an office I had never been in before. Soon after, Mistress Raven and Mistress Brooke and a woman I had never seen before arrived and entered the office. They closed the door. I assumed the woman was my new owner. She was wearing a floral print sundress with red high heels. She was carrying a red handbag. She had curly blond hair and wore too much perfume. But it smelled nice. In fact, it smelled expensive. The door opened after a while and Mistress Brooke asked me to come inside.

As soon as I was in the room, Mistress Brooke closed the door behind me. The office was large inside. There was a desk with chairs in front of it about 20 feet from the door. The wall behind the desk had three large windows that looked out over the entrance to the building, and in fact, I could see the main gate and drive onto the property.

"12." Mistress Raven said seated behind the desk "You have broken a record. You already have been a rare case from the beginning. You have set standards in your training, and you display all of the qualities we want from everyone who graduates here. You truly are to be commended. This is Madam Jesse. She is your new owner as of right now. Stand up and say hello to her, 12." I stood up and took her hand and brought it to my lips and kissed it softly. "Thank you, Ma'am." I said to her, keeping my eyes low as I did so. "The pleasure is all mine, I am sure." She said in a heavy southern accent. She had a sweet voice. Thick and sweet like molasses. Mistress Laura stood up from her chair and came over to me and gave me a hug. "I am going to miss you, 12. Please take care of yourself." she turned and walked out of the room. I started to tear up a little. Mistress Brooke stood and in her super chipper high pitched voice she told me to be good and to have fun. She slapped my ass and walked out the door too, leaving me there with Mistress raven and with Madam Jesse. "Have a seat in this chair, 12." Mistress Raven instructed me motioning to the chair in front of her that Mistress Laura had been sitting in. It was still warm. Warm from her. I reveled in that. I looked directly at Mistress Raven.

"12. You have sold for more money than any other slave here has ever been sold for in the past. You set a record. As a surrender, who paid his fees up front, fifty percent of the sales price go to you. Madam Jesse just paid three hundred and fifty thousand dollars for you. Twenty percent goes to your training Mistress, and the balance will go to the academy." As Mistress Raven was talking, I turned to look at Madam Jesse with my mouth hanging open. She was all smiles. "I had no idea about the record." She poured her words slowly like pancake syrup. "But it makes no never mind anyhow, I was going to buy you if it went twice that price. I don't lose at auctions, and money ain't the point. Getting what I want is the point. Don't you think?" Her question hung in the air like cigar smoke. "Yes Ma'am." I responded, smiling back to her. "Darlin, you are to just call me Jess. Everybody calls me Jess. Okay?" she really did seem super nice. I could get used to that accent, too. It really put me at ease.

"We will be setting up a trust with your money, 12. You will have access to it in 365 days, if your new owner allows you personal money. But you surely will not need it. The terms of the contract you both will be signing state that the owner shall provide for you in all areas. Also, it is worth mentioning that we do not just let someone take you, never to be seen again. There will be random checks to make certain that they are living up to the contract, and that you are in good health. Additionally, if you are to run off, or commit a crime, or refuse to perform for any reason, you will be in breach of contract. You void your share of the money and it will be returned to the purchaser. Does that all sound reasonable to you, 12?" she was looking at me with a completely blank face. "Yes, Mistress Raven." Is the only thing I could think to say. "Honey, you just don't have a thing to worry about, everything is going to be just fine. Let's just get all this paperwork behind us now so we can get on down the road today. Okay?" Jess had a manner of speech and her thick accent made me feel like I was being hugged with her words. I smiled at her and she took that as an agreement and said: "Okay then. Here you go 12, I got you some clothes to wear on my way here. I can't exactly take you to the airport like that. You poor thing, bless your heart. Here put these on." And Jess handed me a bag. I could see she had the chain with the keys to my chastity cage around her neck.

I put on the clothes she gave me, a pair of blue jeans, a Pull over shirt, and some socks and sneakers. We both signed four or five times and Mistress Raven had a Notary come in and stamp it all. Jess got copies for both of us and before you knew it, we were on our way to the limousine she had waiting to drive us to the airport. I watched out the back window as we drove away. I never saw Mistress Laura, or the academy, ever again.

The drive back to the airport was filled with a strange mix of sensations of excitement, apprehension, gratitude and of fear. Yes fear. I was afraid of the unknown, and not fully trusting of this woman in the backseat with me, who spoke in English, but in a foreign manner. She didn't say anything for a while. Then she put her hand on my leg. "I really liked the way you answered that interviewer lady. You know, the one from the video today? I really liked the way you answered her questions. Were you taught to answer like that?" The pitch of her voice rose at the end of every question. I supposed it was some kind of signal to people who weren't really listening that she was asking a question, or something. "No Ma'am. I answered honestly. I was taught to be open and to be honest." I hoped that she didn't take that the wrong way.

"I just think that there should be more men like you. I really do. Are you hungry Darlin? I bet your hungry, let's pull over and get us a bite before we get to the airplane." And like that she told the driver to stop at the next burger joint.

I was hungry. My stomach was cramping a little bit. We arrived at a nice-looking steak house outside of Reno called "Bronco's". We headed inside and were seated in a booth. A menu was placed in front of each of us. I wasn't sure what I was supposed to do. I thought that it might be faster than explaining to just ask her to order for me, but she was in front of me on that. She just picked up the menus and handed them back to a waitress and said: "We will each have a cheeseburger, fries and Iced tea, thank you." And the waitress nodded and disappeared, returning very soon thereafter with two ice teas.

"Do you have any questions for me, Darlin? I would expect you have some questions." She asked me sweetly. "Yes Ma'am. How should I address you? As Madam or as my Mistress?" I asked her. "Oh Sugar, just call me Jess. Everybody calls me Jess. I am not really into the whole 'Mistress' thing anyhow. I know women who are, and it is fun and all, but I think you should just call me Jess. Okay, Sweetie? "Okay, Jess." I answered and smiled. She put her hand on my hand and she smiled at me.

When the food arrived, it smelled wonderful. I ate my burger in record time, like a competition eater. I had not had a meal like that for a long time, and it tasted pretty damned good, too. She had watched me while I ate. She ate too, but really only a few bites of her burger. She paid the bill, and we were back in the car. The limo driver had opened the car door for us, something I had planned to do for her. She told the driver to continue taking us to the airport. I had wondered what time our flight was, but I didn't ask. As it happened, I didn't even know what time it was. As we drove along, I looked out the window. I thought to myself I had not really known what time it was for a long time. Time was meaningless to a slave. For all of the stress a slave endured over timing, what time it actually was meant nothing at all unless there was a task to be done at a certain time. Being free from the need to keep up with time, was an underappreciated freedom that I would bet few people enjoyed. I smiled. Jess had been watching me, and she asked me "What are you smiling at, 12?". Her accent was actually quite sexy. "I was wondering what time our flight was and realized I didn't even know what time it is. I thought that was funny." I told her, looking her in the eye, which was weird too. I had not had this much eye contact with a woman in a long time. Very rarely. "Oh Sugar, you're so funny. Maybe I need to buy you a watch. Now it's a little before two o'clock in the afternoon, and it don't matter anyhow because our flight leaves whenever we get there, it's my plane." And she laughed at herself and put her hand on my leg as she said it. I laughed a little, too. I didn't want to tell her, but I really didn't want a watch.

Just like rock stars in a music video, the limo pulled directly up to the private jet that sat there waiting for us at the airport. We boarded the plane, and the pilot closed the door before walking into the cabin.

"Good afternoon, Jess. I see you have a companion with you, Sir, my name is Sean Pearson. Jess calls me Captain Sean." He extended his hand to me. I took his hand and I said, "Nice to meet you, I'm 12." Before he could ask me about my name being 12, Jess butted in and changed the subject on him. "Captain Sean, could you please get us in the air as soon as you can, please." He simply nodded his head and went to the cockpit and started his procedure for getting us in the air.

The airplane was fancy! There were two overstuffed seats facing each other on each side of the aisle. There was a table between them. She got up and went to the galley and returned with a bottle of wine and two glasses. She handed me the bottle and a corkscrew. I opened the bottle and poured the wine into both wine glasses she had put on the table. There was a hole to put the wine bottle in on the table so it wouldn't fall off the table. I noticed the plane was moving when the fasten seatbelts sign lit up. She raised her glass, and I clinked my glass with hers and she said, "Here is to you, 12." We both took a sip of the wine. "Thank you, Jess." I said in response after I swallowed the wine, and I had never had wine like that before. It was very sweet. The engines got louder, and the plane was going fast seemingly all of a sudden. I felt the nose of the plane raise up sharply and saw the ground fall away from the plane thru the window. I was sitting facing Jess, my new owner, with my back to the cockpit. I felt the pull of the Earth as it forced me to lean forward towards the rear of the plane. Towards Jess. I could feel the pressure in my chastity cage being pushed into the seat cushion. I had flown before, but never on a private plane. This was absolutely the best way to fly. Jess was smiling at me. "Texas here we come!" she said loudly and the let out a big "YEEHAA!!!"

Texas. So, we were going to Texas. Jess was smiling at me, and I smiled back. The plane had leveled off and the seatbelt light had gone off. We sipped the wine and she asked if I liked it. "It is very sweet." I told her. I did like it though, as evidenced by my getting another glass full, and refilling hers. "I am very excited to get you to Waco." She told me. I had only ever heard of Waco once before. Some cult members shooting it out with the FBI or something, I couldn't remember the story. I hoped she didn't belong to a cult. She cocked her head like I confused her. "You weren't even going to ask?" she asked me and kind of giggled. "Ask, Ma'am?" I replied. "Ask about what?" Her smile faded ever so slightly. "I told you; it's just 'Jess'. Lay off that 'Ma'am' stuff. Calling me 'Ma'am' makes me feel old." Her smile returned and I said "Sorry, Jess. It's a habit, it implies respect of your authority, not of your age." I turned a little red. I felt embarrassed. "I apologize, Jess." She smiled big, took a sip of her wine. "Ask where we are going." She said. As she spoke, she played with the chain around her neck that held the key to my cage. I felt my cock putting pressure in the cage. "No Ma'am......I mean Jess, I will be wherever you want me. I am at your service. I belong to you." I answered. She smiled, and did not break eye contact as she said "How does that make you feel, 12? Belonging to a woman you have never met before? Being purchased?" she took a sip of her wine. I took a sip of mine as well, "I am happy. Happy that I am wanted. Happy to be at your service." I told her my story and how I came to realize what I was. She played with the chain around her neck as I talked.

Jess had a vineyard someplace west of Waco, Texas. Her huge

farm sprawled for miles in any direction from her three-story mansion. It was beautiful, and just inside the doorway was a grand stairway that circled half the room that opened up to a rotunda that was not visible from the outside. There was a giant pool outside the large bay windows that overlooked the Texas hill country rolling hills, and her grapevines stretching out for what looked like miles. There was not another house in sight. Jess had shown me the whole place, the holding barn where the barrels of wine were aging. The bottling and labeling facility, as well as the shipping dock. She had a full staff that took care of the house, and she explained that nothing was going to be expected of me while I was there. There were even clothes for me to wear in the room she gave to me on the second floor. "You should remain clothed here, during the day, in front of the staff you are a house guest, not a 'slave'. Just enjoy yourself, 12. Enjoy the pool, there is a sauna. Help yourself to anything from the kitchen, and if you want something that isn't there, let Mr. Davis know. He runs the kitchen and the staff. His office is behind the kitchen. He is gone for the day today, but he will be back in the morning. The staff leaves after supper is cleaned up, usually around seven or so unless there is a party. Tonight, we are having fried chicken and all the fixings, I hope you like that."

She really seemed to enjoy showing me everything, and it was all very impressive. I could tell that the house was new, barely lived in. My room had a private bathroom with a whirlpool tub. It had a huge TV and even a video game console. It had its own patio overlooking the pool with nice comfortable furniture that matched the pool furniture. The first thing I did was run me a bath and soak in the tub. I had a soda and plenty of bubbles. This was all genuinely nice, but I missed my Mistress. I wondered what she was doing. I felt alone and disconnected.

I dressed for supper in a pair of jeans that fit me perfectly, and a red pull over shirt that was made of an exceptionally light linen. I made my way to the dining room, but nobody was there. I smelled the fried chicken and followed my nose into the kitchen. Two Hispanic women dressed in white were working and I said hello, they responded with smiles and nods. Jess appeared behind me. "We serve ourselves here, unless it is a formal party. Just grab a plate from the cabinet and the forks are in this drawer here. I was thinking it might be nice to eat poolside, it's a nice evening. What do you think?" She seemed to be excited about that idea so I told her that I thought that would be nice. She asked me if I wanted iced tea, and I said yes. The two women said something to each other in Spanish and took a carafe of tea and two glasses of ice to a table outside. We put fried chicken, mashed potatoes and gravy, fried okra and coleslaw on our plates and grabbed our forks and napkins and headed for the table with the tea glasses on it and sat down. As we ate, she talked about her vineyard, how she is expanding and the distribution of her label. A world that is totally foreign to me. "None of this would have ever happened if it had not been for Queen Melissa. Who knows where I would be if it had not been for her? I can't wait for you to meet her." I nodded, not knowing what to say.

The sun was setting as we finished our supper and she stood up. "I am going to retire for the evening, 12. But you can make yourself at home, do anything you like. I have a busy morning tomorrow, but I will see you in the afternoon. Let's have drinks, okay?" she asked me. "Sounds great, Jess. I would like that very much." The two women from the kitchen came to the table and began taking our dishes. "Okay, Goodnight 12." And she bent down to my cheek and gave it a peck. She turned and went in the house, leaving me at the table which was now clear of dishes.

I went back to my room, and I got nude and crawled under the covers of a giant king size bed. It felt amazing, but that only distracted me for a few minutes from how alone I was for the first time since I drove myself to the airport parking lot and got into that limousine that took me to Mistress Laura. I missed her very much, and even though Jess was very kind, and even though this place was like being at some kind of resort, I would rather be sleeping on the floor next to my Mistress with the taste of her still on my lips. I didn't know if I was going to be able to do this. Act normal and be alone. Why did Jess buy me? Why didn't she want to use me? I told myself that Jess was my owner now. If she wanted me, or if she didn't, it was her decision. Not mine. I was where she wanted me to be, and she knew where I was.

Telling myself that helped. I knew that this wasn't a bad situation. I certainly feared being sold into a worse one. Realizing that calmed me down. But I still cried myself to sleep.

The next morning, I woke up, but I didn't want to get dressed. I felt better nude. I went onto my room's patio and sat in a chair. I watched a worker with a sprayer walking thru the field spraying each grape vine with something. I sat there as long as I could before needing to use the restroom. I took a shower afterwards and styled my hair with some gel that was there. I got dressed in the same clothes that I had worn the night before. I wandered downstairs into the kitchen and found coffee and some doughnuts that tasted delightful. Exploring downstairs, I saw pictures of Jess and a man. He was in every picture with her. Some were in Paris, others in Las Vegas and one in New York. They were embracing each other and looking at the pictures they seemed happy. I noticed a few where the man had lost a lot of weight, and one of them where he was very skinny, and his hair was gone. Jess was in that picture, too. She had a smile, but, she looked like she had been crying. I started to put together that maybe he had gotten sick. I assumed that the man was her husband, and that he must have died. It made me feel bad for her. In that picture I could see the pain in her eyes, even though she was smiling.

Wandering around I felt like I was getting to know her a

little. It was clear that she liked sunflowers. There were pictures of sunflowers, sunflower print on several items, and fresh sunflowers in vases on different tables in different rooms. This woman liked sunflowers. No doubt about it. I gabbed another doughnut and a fresh cup of coffee and went back up to my room. I took off my clothes and got back into bed and took a nap. I held my chastity caged penis and balls as I fell asleep. When I woke up, Jess was sitting on the edge of the bed next to me with her fingers in my hair.

"Good afternoon, sleepy head!" she said laughingly to me as I opened my eyes. "I am surprised you are still in bed!" she said softly.

"I was up earlier but I got bored and took a nap." I told her, feeling a bit embarrassed about it. She wasn't embarrassed. She ran her hands down my chest and pinched each nipple. I was looking her right in the eyes and her smile turned devilish as her hand found its way over my stomach and over my caged cock. I could hear her breathing speed up as she pulled the covers back and then grabbed me by the balls, softly at first, but then more firmly. She was looking at my cock cage and it had started to get tight as the blood was trying to get in. My hands were planted at my sides and my eyes were moving all over her body. The chain which held my key was around her neck. She was wearing a yellow sun dress and it looked very good on her. As if the color yellow was meant just for her. She stood up and removed the dress and she was completely nude. I noticed a scar under her left breast, it was a perfect line about 2 inches long. Her perfect "c" cup breast were implants. They looked beautiful. Her pubic hair was trimmed high above her vagina, and her labia was pursed tightly and pink with just a bit of darkening on the edges. She was a very sexy woman.

She bent down and kissed me as she squeezed my testicles with one hand, she held my face with the other. She licked my lips and bit the lower one before she climbed into the bed and on top of me. Straddling my head with each knee she lowered her pussy onto my mouth. I licked her deeply between her folds and she rose up away from me, then lowered herself back down slowly until my tongue just barely made contact. I began licking her and she lowered down a bit more, then a bit more after a few minutes, and then after a few more minutes she lowered a little more. I enthusiastically licked her pussy bottom to top, then top to bottom. Lapping at her juices. She held on to the large headboard as she started gyrating her hips into the rhythm of my attention to her. She kept lowering herself on to my mouth, rocking her hips faster, using my face to grind her pussy on. Her clit rubbing my nose hard enough to block my air flow, causing me to breath in rhythm to her thrust. Her juices were running into my eyes and down my cheeks. I held her ass cheeks with my hands, and she brought one hand down and got a fist full of my hair. She started grinding harder and I couldn't breathe at all. I held my breath and tapped her on the leg, but she just kept pushing down on my face, which her pussy was now making full travel on, in fast order. I was almost completely out of air and started to wiggle under her when she suddenly tensed up and then exploded in orgasm, screaming as she came and lifting herself off of me, spraying my face with her essence. I gasped for my breath and actually, literally inhaled her juices. She sat back on my chest and looked at me. "Yours is a face I could grow to love, 12." She said in her southern accent. Then she got off of me and put her dress back on. "I'm going to do that a lot!" she said with a giggle and then she left the room without another word.

She meant what she said. She did it a lot. Over the next couple of days, she rode my face at least four more times. She didn't talk about it, she didn't act differently, she just straddled my face and ground her pussy to climax. Once she didn't take her dress off and I was fully clothed. She told me sweetly to lay down next to the pool and she squatted over me. I loved the aroma of her, and the taste of her juices. I smelled her on me around the clock. One time she woke me up in the middle of the night to use me, and I had gotten used to her waking me up literally every morning to use my face.

After a couple of weeks, I overheard her telling someone on the phone about it, her voice echoing down the hallway: "Honestly, I wish I would have gotten one years ago. I don't understand why every woman doesn't have one! You simply must get one of your own." There was a lull as whoever she was talking to talked to her. "We should do that!" She said excitedly "Let's do that! Tomorrow is fine. You call her and I will call Grace." I heard her stomp her foot in excitement. I was in my bedroom dressing, and she ran down the hallway to find me. "We are going to a party, 12. Tomorrow night. It is going to be FUN!" she slipped her hand down the front of my pants and cupped my balls in her hands, her other hand caressed my ass cheek, and she hugged me like that, squeezing my balls. She held me for a minute before removing her hand. "I am going to have you be a slave for a few of my friends. Okay?" She beamed at me when I answered her "Yes, Mistress."

The limo arrived in front of a house in Waco Texas near downtown Waco. The neighborhood was nice, but not what I would call "wealthy". Jess exited the car first on the street side of the car. She was wearing yet another beautiful sun dress. This one was red with black paisley stitchwork all over it. It fit her beautiful shape perfectly, like it was made to fit her. I would not have been surprised to learn that it had, in fact, been made to fit her. That would not be shocking at all. She waited on the side of the car I was on for me to exit the car. I was wearing a white sheer, thigh length bathrobe, and absolutely nothing else. Jess had wanted to make an entrance. She took my hand and led me to the door. As we approached, the door opened revealing three women waiting to receive us. They each had drinks in their hands and smiles on their faces. They all greeted Jess with hugs and one of the women took my hand and led me into a living room. There was a sofa, a love seat, a large chair with an ottoman and a chaise lounge. Quite obviously the coffee table had been removed, and the furniture was situated around a Persian rug. The belt that held my robe closed was untied and my robe was removed from me. I automatically went to my knees and sat up straight with my palms up. "Good Boy." Said the woman who led me into the room and disrobed me. She patted me on the head as she turned and headed for the sofa. Jess walked past me and ran her fingers in my hair before continuing to the love seat. She had shoulder length brown hair that was straight. She looked at me as she sat down, and I remembered to lower my gaze. Jess and the two other women were still talking inside the foyer, and they roared with laughter before coming into the living room.

They all sat down on the sofa together and I could feel them looking at me as the room fell silent. If ever I felt like a bug on a slide in a laboratory, it was then. Jess began talking first "Ladies, this is 12. He will do whatever you ask him to do." Her sugary words flowing casually into the room. "12! Roll over and play dead!" shouted one of the women. I thought that was funny too, and it got a lot of laughter from everyone when I did it for her, rolling onto my side and curled up in a fetal position, laying still. "Good boy, 12!" said the woman. Taking her cue, I rose up on my hands and knees and tried to wag my tail for them the best I could, just to play along for them. They roared with laughter, but I wasn't embarrassed at all. Then Jess said, "come here, 12." And patted the top of her thigh. I remained on my hands and knees and crawled over to Jess. I put my cheek where she patted her leg. I closed my eyes as she ran her fingers thru my hair. She just petted me. Someone slapped my ass and they all giggled. Then I felt a hand on the small of my back as another hand grabbed my cock cage and pulled. "Is this thing really necessary? Seems like an inconvenience if you wanted some dick." Before Jess could answer another of the women did "I like it. You own his dick!" The woman let go of my cock cage and began slapping my ass, hard. Over and over.

Jess grabbed my hair in one hand and lifted my head, pulled up her dress with the other hand, and then plunged my face in between her legs. Again, she wasn't wearing panties and the aroma of her sex intoxicated me. When I got my tongue into the folds of her pussy, I found her to be both hot and wet. The woman slapping my ass finally quit. I could hear them talking softly and one of them left for a moment and returned. Then Jess pulled my head up by my hair and told me to lay on my back in the center of the room. I saw that the other women were now nude. As soon as I was on my back the one with the brown hair that led me into the room got on top of me on her hands and knees and lowered her pussy onto my face. I began licking her up and down. She had an exceptionally large clit. It was engorged and when she focused it on my mouth, I sucked on it as she grinded it into me. I licked it and sucked on it and then she orgasmed. She rose off of me suddenly and was replaced by one of the other women. She also had brown hair, cut short. She was very thin and had small breast. Almost nothing there at all. Mosquito bites, as they say. My cock was straining against its cage as she hovered above my face and grabbed my cock and balls in both hands and pushed down causing me quite a bit of pain before she lowered her totally shaved pussy onto my mouth. My face was already wet, and she slipped and slid herself all over my face. Her pussy tasted very different. More musky, salty. Strong aroma filled my nostril as she rocked her sex on my face using my cock and balls as leverage to push and pull herself on me. She moaned loudly and her body shook and shivered. It felt like she was going to pull my cock right off my body as she orgasmed heavily, but did not slow down. She kept right on grinding on me, and she orgasmed again, this time screaming louder and shaking more violently. She let go of my now aching package and lifted herself off of me. I watched her as she knelt down in front of Jess, and Jess again raised her skirt. The skinny woman plunged her head between Jess's thighs. Jess saw me looking and she smiled as she threw her head backwards in ecstasy.

I watched in awe. Then the blonde woman was standing above me. She bent down and stuffed my mouth full with a rubber plug and she strapped a harness around my head. The plug in my mouth had a dildo on it on the other end. She applied some lube to the dildo, then she squatted over my face. I was thankful that she was facing away from my cock until she grabbed a fist full of my hair and slowly pulled me up as she lowered down onto the dildo. Once she was halfway down, she dropped my head, and my head fell down onto the rug, hard. And she dropped herself completely on the dildo and fucked my face. She humped slowly at first and she thrusted down hard until she was pushing the plug into my mouth. She rode me for a long time speeding up, slowing down. I felt someone's hands on my balls, gently rubbing them. Caressing them, tugging gently on them and my cock cage. I could feel the fingernails stroking firmly and playfully.

The plug in my mouth actually felt good as I bit down on it. My whole mouth was tired from the activities. The woman riding my face was working harder and harder. I loved watching her, watching the dildo disappear inside her and then reappear again. Her juices ran into my nose. Pussy had been the only thing I could smell for over a week before that night. I loved it. I loved providing these women with pleasure. I loved looking at her labia swollen, glistening and red as she orgasmed and stopped moving completely for a few moments, then slid the rest of the way down and bore down on my face. She rocked back and forth a few times while moaning before getting off of me. She sat on the rug next to my head and flicked the dildo back and forth with two fingers.

The fingers stroking my scrotum belonged to the brown hair woman. She poked her long fingernails between the bars of my chastity cage and into the head of my swollen and restrained cock. After Jess climaxed, the women all got dressed. Jess told me not to move. The women all went into the kitchen. I could hear them talking, laughing. I must have fell asleep. I have no idea how much later it was when Jess woke me up. I still had the dildo strapped to my face and I had made quite a mess slobbering all over myself because the plug in my mouth caused me to salivate heavily. She removed the harness and held a finger up to her lips and said "SHHHH" as she pulled the plug from my mouth. She stuck the dildo into a bag. I had to pee so bad it was starting to hurt, and I whispered to her that I needed to pee. "Outside." She said lowly. She put my robe back on me and we quietly went out the front door. Her limo was idling at the curb, and I went behind a hedge and urinated before getting into the car with her. Her makeup was all smudged and her hair was mussed up. I am sure we looked the site. The limo pulled away and we went home. We didn't talk much. She told me I needed a bath. She told me her friend, Queen Melissa, was coming over this weekend, and that I was going to love her.

I felt content and happy. I was living a fantasy lifestyle. I was happy Jess bought me. I didn't know what was in front of me. But I wasn't bothered by what was behind me anymore. True, I was a slave. I was owned. But I had never felt so free to be happy ever before.

My Queen deserves this from me, and more.

1. I will serve, obey, and above all, seek to please my Queen in all things.
2. I will not hesitate to obey my Queen, hesitation is disobedience.

All tasks and orders will be performed with expediency.

3. I will promptly respond when spoken to. Speaking clearly and concisely. All yes or no answers will be followed by " My Queen, My love, My Darling, or My Beautiful Wife (if in mixed company).

4. The needs of my Queen must always come before mine and I must always be attentive to those needs.

5. I will actively listen to my Queen only when she is speaking to me, and not interrupt my Queen whenever she is talking, no matter who she is talking to.

6. I must accept all praise humbly and always carry myself with dignity. I am honored to be chosen by my Queen and must never shame her. I am not to ever hang my head or otherwise avoid eye contact (unless told to), even when being corrected.

7. My Queen's caution and safe words are available to me at any time. But they come with a price to be decided by my Queen.

8. I choose willingly to be my Queen's property, and I will wear her mark.

9. In being my Queen's property I am her most valuable asset and must take care of myself as well as I take care of any of her toys. My physical appearance is the perfect expression of my love for my Queen.

10. While my Queen's word is law, I am expected to make decisions in whatever capacity I am allowed. A totally reliant sub is a lazy one.

11. I must never allow myself to become passive in my submission to my Queen and must continuously seek active ways in which to please her.

12. I will wear my cage at all times unless needed by my Queen or otherwise directed by my Queen to remove it for hygiene or health purposes. My Queen alone will hold the key, which she may display.

13. My limits will be respected, and all requests will be considered, but I will trust in my Queen, who is the final say in all things. She

knows best.

14. I must never question my Queen. Questioning is a form of disrespect if not done with absolute politeness and prior permission.

15. I will be available for my Queen's use as often as she desires through task, sex, or amusement. My Queen is free to use my body as she pleases. I have no say in how she may use me. Punishment is included in this, of which I must submit graciously.

16. When I do not do my chores at home to my Queen's satisfaction, she will punish me.

17. If I interrupt my Queen, I will be punished.

18. My Queen will punish me any time she may want, even if I do not deserve it, because I have to remember my place.

19. I will thank my Queen before and after a punishment.

20. I am obedient, docile, and listen to what my Queen says at all times.

My Queen knows what I want, and it is my complete submission and obedience to her.

21. I will hold open all doors for my Queen.

22. I will not walk in front of my Queen.

23. I will carry all bags or items for my Queen, including her purse if requested.

24. I will write, and I will memorize a Mantra, which must be to my Queen's approval. I will recite my Mantra to her each night and whenever requested by her.

25. I will redeem myself for not adhering to these rules in the past by living by them without fail from today on.